AMERICAN NINJA

Brett Wallace is a man about San Francisco, a lover of good women, good food, and good theater, in that order. He's also skilled in Japan's deadly art of the Ninja, a force so destructive it can only be taught to that rarest of human beings—the wise and the good.

Brett Wallace will fight only when he has to. And when he fights—he kills.

Books by Wade Barker

Ninja Master #1: Vengeance Is His
Ninja Master #2: Mountain of Fear

Published by
WARNER BOOKS

NINJA MASTER
#1
VENGEANCE IS HIS

Wade Barker

WARNER BOOKS

A Warner Communications Company

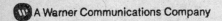

NINJA MASTER
#1
VENGEANCE
IS HIS

Chapter 1

"May I have your attention please," said Simon Ashford tapping his glass with a spoon and raising his booming authoritative voice so that it could be heard above the din of some twenty to thirty eating, drinking, and socializing guests.

The party was in full swing by this time, about nine. Though it was not formal, the gathering was peopled with the well-dressed and moneyed, Simon's friends from a lifetime of unusually good luck and considerable success. An ex-mayor of the city, the current D.A., several doctors, about a half dozen contractors, a couple of lawyers and an accountant were among those tipping their glasses in the splendor of the Ashford home. Located in Upper Arlington, the house was a showcase of contemporary design with windows looking out on the city and, on the other side of the house, windows looking out upon a floodlit forest which was part of the considerable acreage owned by Ashford. This was the house Simon and his wife Marian had wanted all their lives. Six years ago it had become a reality.

It had been a blow to Simon when his son Brett had wanted to become a philosophy major. After graduating from Ohio State three years ago, Brett had gone to Tibet and then Tokyo.

"You don't see a hell of a lot of ads for a philosopher nowadays, for chrissake!" Simon was known to say this on more than one occasion.

A year ago Brett had met Kyoko, decided to marry and return to the States and to Simon's business. Brett's news that he wanted to marry and settle down was greeted with considerable enthusiasm by Simon and Marian. And to have the woman of his choice turn out to be a person of Kyoko's quality exceeded even their fondest hopes. So tonight was the culmination of many dreams for Simon and his wife. They were very proud indeed.

"May I have your attention, please," Simon repeated.

Gradually the crowd stilled and all attention focused on Simon. He motioned for his son and daughter-in-law to join him and he took his wife's hand and pulled her close to him.

"Friends—and everyone here in this room I *do* consider a good friend—I have some news to share with you that makes Marian and I very happy. Most of you here have known our family for a number of years and therefore you know my son. Then you must also know of my *mild* displeasure"—Simon paused here for emphasis—"with his decision to waste what I know to be considerable business talents—inherited mostly from his father's side—and go off and live as a monk on some god-forsaken mountain in a country most geography teachers haven't even heard of. Well, as you also know, the boy came to his senses—which means that he saw things my way, finally.

"Anyhow, all this bull aside, my son is home—where I hope he feels he belongs. And he has become everything his mother and I ever hoped he would be." Simon stopped here for a second as something seemed to stick in his throat. He swallowed hard and continued. "If the truth be known, he's a hell of a lot *more* than we hoped he'd be because he sees things a little more clearly than the old man. But don't let me hear any of *you* saying that."

The crowd laughed politely at the remark and Simon used the opportunity to put his arm around his son, while Marian put her arm around Kyoko and the four stood as one, close in every way.

"So," Simon continued, "I have an announcement to make. Next week for Thanksgiving, our family, the four of us, will have a great deal to be thankful for. But next year, we'll be even more thankful because we'll be setting another place for turkey. Thanks to these two," he said indicating Brett and Kyoko.

The crowd gave the family a hearty applause, and many toasts to the couple were offered during the next hour.

Finally, about midnight, the party began breaking up and by one there were only about four people besides Brett, his folks, and Kyoko. Ed Bracken, an old friend of Simon's was still ready to dance with the lamp in the corner when Simon offered to let him stay in the guest room. Bracken declined because he was expecting an overseas call early in the morning and didn't want to chance missing it.

"But I'm not going to let you drive home, old man. Not in your condition."

"But Simon, I'm f-fine . . . just like a clock. Did I say clock? I meant rock . . . steady as a . . . rock. Yes, that's it. A rock. May I have another drink, Simon?"

"No, no, that's quite enough for tonight. And I'm going to drive you home."

"I'll drive him home, Father, I think you've had a few too many yourself," said Brett entering the room with a plastic trash bag ready to empty ashtrays and pick up other party debris.

"Okay. I'll help your mother and Kyoko. You know where he lives?"

"Unless he moved since I was a kid."

"Nope. Same place. That's about a twenty-minute drive each way. So we'll see you back here in about an hour."

Bracken proved to be a slightly unwieldy character and talked endlessly of Brett's childhood and how he remembered the youngster playing baseball, football, Brett's dating period, and how happy Simon must be to have Brett back home again—"and married yet."

Bracken's wife had died a few years back and the man lived alone in a big old house. Brett made sure Bracken got up to bed all right, then drove directly home.

All the way back he couldn't help but think how lucky he was, how his life had come almost full circle. He was home now, in more ways than one. He remembered this afternoon especially warmly. He'd gone out to buy Kyoko's evening corsage. The fall in Columbus, Ohio, was pretty. The new sweater Kyoko had bought him felt good against his skin. It was just right for the temperature; the highs now vacillated between fifty and sixty degrees. His mind was on pleasant sights and sounds as he negotiated the scenic road in his new Celica, a gift his father had given him when Brett and Kyoko had returned from Tokyo.

That was about a year ago and Brett had made the adjustment much better than he had thought he would. After all, working in his father's real estate development business wasn't exactly what Brett had had in mind when he'd gone to Tibet. Brett was hungry to learn. He'd wanted to know answers to questions most people believed were unanswerable.

His first stop had been Tibet and Master Sanawananda. Brett had studied Eastern Philosophy at Ohio State and had been impressed with Sanawananda's teachings. In Tibet Brett had walked with, talked with, and studied with the master for eight months.

The gray Celica had sped past a pile of leaves near the highway and sent them swirling into the air.

Brett had wondered then what Kyoko's autumn memories were. Last fall they were both in Tokyo preparing to leave for the States.

Meeting Kyoko had changed Brett's life entirely. Before her, there was just the single-minded pursuit of the "great answers." Brett had thought it strange at the time that he had found in her—to him, an unexpected source—enough of the answers to totally redirect his course in life.

The couple had been introduced while Brett was a guest lecturer at the University of Tokyo. His former roommate at Ohio State was teaching full-time there and he had asked Brett to come over and teach for six months and stay with him.

Kyoko was the sister of a friend of Brett's old classmate. At first Brett and Kyoko would only sit and talk about philosophy for hours. Their relationship had deepened gradually. They had developed a taste for each other—the subtleties, the nuances, the differences, the similarities.

Then one afternoon on a hill overlooking the city, Brett had presented Kyoko with a haiku poem he had written for her, only to discover that she had written him one as well. In fact, both poems were romantic declarations of love. Brett and Kyoko had gone back that afternoon to Brett's room and made love repeatedly for the next two days. He had never felt that way before, nor had she. And Brett realized he had found one of *the* answers.

That had been the beginning. A few months later the couple made plans to marry and Brett decided to take a lucrative job with his father's company back in Columbus.

That had been a year ago and since then life had been more joyful and rich than Brett had ever imagined possible. Last week Kyoko had brought Brett the news that she was pregnant. The news was soon passed on to Brett's parents who insisted on having the party to announce the event to the world. Brett and Kyoko would have preferred to be a little more conservative about the whole thing but Brett's mother would not have it any other way. And what was the harm? thought Brett. It seemed to make his folks so happy. In fact, it made Brett and Kyoko happy, too.

Brett felt a profound sense of satisfaction, love and contentment as he pulled into the driveway at about two a.m. He used the electronic door-opener in his father's car to raise the garage door and he parked the car.

He entered the house through the kitchen door which led directly into the garage. That's odd. He figured the dishes would be done by this time. But there were still stacks of them in the sink.

And there was silence. At that moment a strange animal instinct surged within him. Somehow, *he knew*.

"Kyoko!" he screamed as he ran from the kitchen into the living room which now resembled the setting of a ghoulish red nightmare. He screamed repeatedly, not out of fear, but because of repulsion, horror, and disbelief at the sight before his eyes.

Chapter 2

"Oh God, Oh God, Oh God," he kept saying to himself as he fell to his knees, doubling over and retching on the floor. He continued to vomit and moan for several minutes as his mind adjusted to the sickening vision.

Brett looked upon the mass of bloody flesh that was once his mother, his father, and his wife. Slowly he crawled to Kyoko and shut her eyes. There was no doubt she was dead. In a way, Brett was glad. She was at peace. Now. Her nude body had been ravaged sexually and dry brown blood was mixed with some still flowing red blood between her thighs. A look of terror was etched hard as stone on her face. He untied his wife's hands from the legs of the coffee table, and took an afghan from the sofa and covered her. He collapsed, sobbing on her chest.

Each moment of gruesome discovery seemed endless. His mother and father were barely recognizable. His mother's arms and one of his father's legs had been cut off and his father had been decapitated. Vomiting again, Brett collected the pieces and put them back in their right places like a grisly puzzle.

It was then, for the first time, that the thought occurred to him that the killers might still be in the house. For a moment, he wished they were, so that they could kill him too and put him out of his misery.

Then Brett picked up an elongated figurine lying close to Kyoko's body which he presumed had been used to ravage her body and clutched it like a weapon. His mood had changed. He wished that the intruders were still in the house so that he could kill each of them slowly and in the most painful way possible. That became his only goal in life, for he could not see beyond the tragedy, beyond the sights, smells, and deathly stillness around him. He wanted those responsible. He had to kill them. *Had to kill them. Had to kill them. Had to kill them.*

He raced through the house screaming and slashing at shadows with the statuette. Eventually he came to the room he had occupied as a boy and later as a young man. There were the pictures of himself and his father in their baseball uniforms, he and his mother at his high school graduation, pennants of his favorite sports teams, trophies he had received for his many martial arts accomplishments. And there, above them all, scrawled in blood were the words: *Singin' in the Rain.*

The world seemed to drain of color, perceptions clashed in eerie slow motion, and a merry-go-round of madness engulfed Brett as he dropped the figurine and fell, as if parachuting from a plane, into a kind of darkness he had never known.

When Brett regained consciousness, a burly man in a tweed sports coat was leaning over him calling his name. As the fog began to clear, Brett could see a man he recognized standing behind the first man and several other men and one woman milling about either in the bedroom or out in the hall.

"Brett?"

"Yeah," he said, but he wasn't sure. As it all started to come back, he wasn't sure he wanted to return to the nightmare.

"Brett, I'm Sergeant Wilcox. You seem to be okay, son. Pretty lucky from what we can see."

Brett didn't feel lucky.

"My God, Brett," said the second man, a neighbor, moving closer to him, "What in God's name happened here?"

Brett sat up and took a glass of water from another man, a policeman Brett surmised, and drank it down. "Nothing in *God's* name," said Brett.

"We heard screaming about fifteen minutes ago," said

14

James Grady, the neighbor. "I called the police and we came right over."

"Look, Mr. Ashford," said the sergeant, "there are a few things we know and a hell of a lot we don't. For example, where were you when all this was going on?"

Brett took a deep breath and tried to clear his head enough to give the right answers. "I took a friend of my father's home because he was too drunk to drive."

"And the man's name?"

"Ed Bracken. He lives about twenty minutes from here. His address is in the book."

"Why didn't your father drive him home?"

"My father had had a few drinks himself and I just off . . . hey, what he hell . . ." Brett started to get up and move toward the policeman, but his strength didn't allow it.

"For Christ's sake, sergeant!" yelled Grady.

"Okay, okay," appeased Wilcox. "I'm outta line. Look, I may seem to be some kinda hard-ass to you, but I've never seen any goddamned shit like this. I want the bastard who did this and I want him off the fuckin' streets now! And I mean *right* now!"

Brett dropped his head and lowered it into the palms of his hands and massaged his temples with his fingers. "I want him, or them, or it, too," said Brett. "What have you got so far?"

"It looks like a burglary," said Wilcox. "The place seems to have been looted of valuables, at least the kind you can carry in a couple table cloths."

"But why the other . . . the . . ." Brett's pain would not allow him to finish the sentence.

"I don't know, son. I swear to God, I just don't know. The only thing we can figure is maybe they were on something, some drug. Hell, I don't know. But two things I promise you: one, we'll find who did this: and two, they're gonna die.

"I'll make sure the whole damned world knows what kind of garbage we're dealing with. And they'll . . . ah shit!" grunted Wilcox and got up and walked out of the room.

The long night turned into a long morning and Brett refused to leave his bedroom until the carnage had been cleaned up, the bodies removed, police tests made. Grady stayed with him through the night and the Franklin County D.A., Edward Clayton, who had been at the party earlier, arrived on the scene about three saying the kinds of things people say when nothing really can come close to a gruesome situation. But Clayton *also* promised to bring those responsible to justice.

About ten the next morning Clayton drove Brett home. But they just drove on past Brett's house because the entire block was crawling with reporters.

So they went to Clayton's house where his wife took Brett under a motherly wing. Mrs. Clayton knew enough to say nothing except with her eyes, for which Brett was grateful. She led him up to the guest room where he passed out and slept till about eight p.m.

"So where do we go from here, Ted?" asked Brett as he just dallied with a late supper prepared by Mrs. Clayton.

"I talked with Wilcox about an hour ago, and just before that I talked with Chief Bolger. As far as they're concerned there's only one investigation in the whole damned city going on. Partly because everyone knew your folks, partly because of the way it was done. Everybody wants those bastards. I've never seen a manhunt like the one Wilcox has mounted for this thing."

"You say 'those.' Have the police determined there was more than one person?"

"Yes. They believe there were three people involved. They base that on the fact that they found footprints near the driveway leading to and from the house. The prints had been badly trampled upon, however."

"What do you think the chances of finding these bastards really are, Ted?"

"Honestly, I think they're good. Very good, in fact. Don't worry about that. We'll handle this thing from here on. You just concern yourself with getting your life back on track again. Jenny and I are here for you, Brett, and so are a lot of people. Hell, the phone rings continually with people trying to find out if you're okay, and if you need anything. You've got friends, Brett. Use them. They want to help."

"I appreciate everything you've done. But I think I'll

go back home tomorrow. One favor I would ask. If you have any clout with the news media, keep them away for a few days until I'm centered a little more."

"Consider it done. I'll do it even if I have to assign security guards to stand at your door—and I might have to."

"I wonder what they expect me to say. They'll just ask me how I feel about what's happened. How in the hell do they think I feel? Does it satisfy some morbid curiosity to see my hurt up close?"

Later that evening, in Clayton's study, Brett talked with the D.A.

"Brandy?"

"Thanks. I could probably use it."

The D.A. poured them each a snifter of Remy Martin, handed the already seated Brett one glass and sat down opposite him with the other.

"I feel differently, Ted. About a lot of things."

"You'll get squared around again when this thing passes, Brett," said Clayton as he rolled the brandy in the glass and savored its aroma.

"Maybe. Maybe not. Maybe its just growth. Maybe there's no going back. Just like when you start dating, you don't want to go back to spending much time with the guys." Brett paused and took a sip of liquor.

"We never talked much about my stay in Tokyo, did we?"

"No."

"There's something on my mind. I'm not sure how it relates to anything right now, but it would do me good just to talk about it."

"I'm here."

"You know I've been involved in the martial arts since I was eight years old. You used to come and watch me perform at tournaments. And you used to kid me about my meditating every day. I've built my life around being centered, calm, and focused in a world that was otherwise chaotic.

"I met an old man while I was in Tokyo. His name isn't important, but I can tell you that he and I became very close. Have you ever heard of the Ninja?"

"No, can't say as I have."

"It will suffice to say that they are renowned as the most skilled fighting men ever to have existed on this planet. The Samurai would go to these fighters—who for one reason or another were outcasts—to learn advanced fighting techniques.

"Their origin is of little consequence. What is relevant is that this man I met was a highly ranked member of that organization. One night, about a week before I left Tokyo, he took me to one of their secret training centers. I was impressed. Even though I'm quite knowledgeable about the martial arts, nothing I'd ever been exposed to came close to what I saw there.

"That night the old man and I talked. I told him that even though I was impressed, I could not go along with the idea that his men and their talents were for hire. I told him that even revenge was not a suitable provocation. That in the immediate defense of one's self or one's family, I could see it, but to plan a revenge or to be a glorified 'hit man' was something I could never condone. I said that a man who is truly centered understands that the law of karma is greater and truer than the uncertain hand of the avenger."

"And?"

"I don't think I believe that anymore."

"You've just been through a great deal, Brett. Naturally you would feel that way; anybody would. It'll pass, you'll see."

"Maybe, Ted."

"Look Brett, I know you're upset, and we all want these butchers almost as much as you do, but let the authorities do it. Don't become a one-man vigilante group. Promise me that, Brett."

"I can't promise anything right now, Ted. There's too much pain, too much going on inside me to think clearly. Dammit Ted, there's something so unjust about people doing such despicable things to other people and getting away with it. And the law, that's a laugh. What's gonna happen to these bastards? Sure, you and I would like to see them strung up. But sure as I'm sitting here they'll do some time and people will forget. Who knows, maybe in ten years they can play on the phenomenal media blitz this town is bound to give their trial and go on TV, smile in front of the cameras, and people will say, 'By God, they look like nice enough characters. They look like they're sorry.' And they'll be out on the street again. The problem is, these goddamned do-gooders didn't see my family butchered like meat for a barbecue. That's not justice, Ted. By God, it just *isn't justice!*" said Brett, his voice getting louder to emphasize his last words.

Clayton tried to stem Brett's fury with the professional logic of a D.A.

"But we have a system, Brett."

"That system doesn't work anymore, Ted. I mean, sure you can get screwed if you're just some average Joe who doesn't know how to make the law work for you. But if you're a hardened criminal, your best friend is the law. I tell you, there's something wrong with that, Ted. Something very wrong and people aren't going to stand for it forever."

"And what does that mean?"

"I don't know. But I feel something. I felt it before this thing with my folks and Kyoko happened. I just tried to ignore it. But you can't ignore it. Nobody is untouched by what's happening here in this country, now. And people, good people, people who pay the freight for the freeloaders and the criminals, are going to reach a breaking point. There's going to come a time when there's nothing left to protect anymore unless people start taking care of themselves."

"That's what the police are for. It's what my job is all about."

"I'm not putting down the police, or you for that matter. The police can't be everywhere at once. Offenders are hardly likely to wait for the police to arrive, before they proceed with a crime. No, the power and responsibility for one's safety and well-being and that of one's family has got to be taken by the individual himself."

"I know what you're saying, Brett, but—"

"Do you, Ted? Do you? I mean where is the justice and sanity in a situation where some guy who owns a house has got to wait for some other guy to set fire to it before he can try to defend it? And even at that, he better make sure the offender is of legal age or else he might be getting into serious trouble himself for striking a minor. Man, if a person is old enough to commit a crime, set fire to my house, rape my wife, then by God, he's old enough to take the consequences. Where's the justice in a guy beating up another guy so bad the victim loses his job, his wife, his house, while the mugger goes to jail and collects checks from the government while doing time?"

"What can I say, Brett?"

"Say it stinks, Ted. Say it's a farce, a bad joke on people who grew up being taught they were supposed to play by the rules."

"You're right. But you're wrong, too. The system works a lot of the time. What would we do without it? There would be chaos."

"You think there's respect for law and order? What do you think we've got now?"

"I've dedicated my life to the law, Brett. I still have faith in it. It doesn't always work, but it's all we've got. And, even though I know you don't believe it now, it will work in this case and you will *have* justice. I swear to God that I will do everything in my power to see to it."

"I know you'll try. Hey, maybe we both ought to sleep on this," said Brett lifting his glass in a final toast.

"To your mom and dad and Kyoko," said Ted.

"To my family . . . and justice for what was done to them."

The two men finished their drinks, said good night, and went to bed.

Chapter 3

"I've hired a couple of security guards, friends of mine, to help keep people away for a few days," said Clayton as he pulled into Brett's driveway and into the garage.

"I appreciate it."

"Just try to rest for a few days. Get your strength back. I'll take care of the funeral arrangements if you want."

"No thanks. That's my responsibility and I'll handle it. Besides, I know Ed Polamo. He and my folks were friends. Dad and I talked about what to do when he and Mom died. He told me he'd already told Ed the kind of arrangements to provide and Ed would take care of everything."

"If you change your mind, the offer still stands."

"I know, Ted. Thanks. You and Jenny have been very kind. I don't know how to thank you. But I'm much better now. Not the same as before, but I'll be all right. Really."

"Okay. But I'll give you a call this evening just to see how you're doing. But there's something else, Brett."

"Yes?"

"That talk we had last night. I hope you reconsider. Give it time. Okay?"

"Sure."

"So I'll call you tonight."

Brett got out of the car and went into his house. Ted drove away and two guards took up their positions. Both were dressed casually, one in a sports coat, the other in a scarlet and gray Ohio State jacket. The guy in the sports coat sat just inside the garage, which was open, so he could stop anyone coming to the front door. The guy in the jacket sat in a lawn chair just outside the back door. Their guns were not visible, but Ted had assured Brett that the men were armed. Just in case. For a long moment, Brett wished the guards would go away and the beasts who had killed his family would come after him. Brett knew that with his fifteen years of martial arts training under his belt, he could kill each of them more slowly and painfully than they could possibly imagine. He could do it. And for the first time in his life, Brett thought, he *would* do it.

The fish tank gurgled tranquilly as Brett began to sort through the heap of mail sitting on the coffee table. People wanted him to know that they felt his pain. He *knew* they didn't—how *could* they? But he appreciated the thought. Most of all, people just wanted him to know they cared. There were a dozen or so telegrams from out of state. People had heard about it, and wanted to assert their outrage.

Brett was ready to explode with anger, but he didn't know how. For all his bitterness and need to strike out at someone —something—in his heart, he hoped Ted was right. He hoped that the system, Ted's system, could mete out justice. In a way, Brett wanted to be wrong about the views he expressed to Ted. There would be a measure of comfort to know that the system still worked. Brett desperately needed to see and touch and sense familiar things, to know that there was some sanity left in the world. That criminals weren't *really* in charge here. Without this knowledge, Brett knew that his life could never be the same.

The house was more than half empty that night when Brett finally decided to call it a day. The second shift of guards had arrived, Brett had greeted them. It was too late to call anyone. There was no avoiding it now.

He had two choices. He could sleep on the couch, hide all the pictures of Kyoko and his folks, put away all the favorite items Kyoko treasured and which were attached to beautiful memories. There was, in each recollection, a definite pang of fear he felt in the pit of his stomach when he came upon something or entered a room in the house he hadn't gone into since the incident. Was it possible there would be something in that room that would tear him apart?

But one aspect of Brett that remained constant, even through the tragedy, was that he didn't back off from a confrontation. He knew he'd have to face things sooner or later, it might as well be now. He didn't want to hide Kyoko's beauty, her profound influence on his life.

And he didn't.

Next to the night of the tragedy itself, this was the toughest night of Brett's life.

For the next few days the papers were full of the stuff. "Informed sources" talked of police theories. Some of the more gruesome details were "leaked" to the press. The whole city was abuzz with thoughts and feelings about the murders. The incident created wide-spread fears as people now realized that it could happen to them, that something had to be done before it did.

About a week later Brett held a no questions-allowed news conference at which he read a prepared statement. He thanked the hundreds of people who had written to him and, going against strong emotions writhing up inside him, called for cool heads to prevail and to let justice take its course.

One night after Brett had just finished meditating—which he was now doing twice a day instead of once—he got a call from Ted.

"Brett, I've got some news."

"Tell me," said Brett with the feeling of hairs on his arm and the back of his neck standing on end in anticipation.

"They've got 'em, Brett. Wilcox just brought them in."

The words left Brett stunned. What should he do?

He took a deep breath and sighed. "What do I do, Ted?"

"Nothing tonight. They're going to be arraigned tomorrow morning downtown."

"I want to be there."

"I don't know, Brett. Do you know what you're letting yourself in for?"

"No. But I know I should be there."

"I don't know . . ."

"Will you be there?"

"Yeah, but . . ."

"When are you planning to leave for the courthouse?"

"I've got to do a few things at the office, so I'll leave home about eight . . ."

"See you about seven-thirty. I'll have some coffee with you," said Brett and hung up. He wasn't sure he was doing the right thing, but he was sure he couldn't do anything else.

"You can always back out," said Ted as he pulled into his parking space behind the courthouse and turned off the ignition.

"I'm going through with it, Ted. I appreciate your trying to shield me from more pain, but I want to be there. To do what, I don't know. Remember our talk that night at your house about justice and injustice?"

"Yes."

"I just want to be there to see that things don't get screwed up somehow. I don't have a lot of faith in leaving things to other people. I just want to be there, Ted. More than anything I will at least *feel* like I'm doing something."

"Okay, Brett. Come into my office and wait for me to prepare a few things, then we'll go downstairs together."

The first Brett saw of them was the back of their heads. They looked as though they hadn't taken a bath in some time. They were all dressed in jeans. Two had on leather jackets and the third was wearing a blue work shirt. It was all Brett could do to control himself. Not ten yards from where he sat in the courtroom stood the men who raped his wife and butchered his family. He felt himself getting sick. He tried to meditate, to center himself on the single thought of control. For the most part, it worked.

Pleas of not guilty were entered and the whole proceeding lasted just a few minutes. As the three were led from the courtroom by guards, they laughed and mugged for cameras.

As Ted and Brett walked from the courtroom, Ted was stopped by another man and pulled aside for a whispered conversation. The man walked away and Ted turned back to Brett looking worried.

"What is it Ted?"

He hesitated, then said, "Nothing, really."

"Come on, Ted. No secrets."

"It looks like Quentin Levy is going to get involved in the case."

Brett had heard the name. Who hadn't? Quentin Levy was one of the best defense lawyers in the country.

"Why?"

"Notoriety. Why else? Levy's a real bleeding heart and he wants to make sure we small-towners don't get carried away with our emotions and turn into a lynch mob."

"What does this mean, Ted? You're worried; I can tell."

"It's just that Levy is known for pulling all kinds of tricks, and not necessarily in the public's best interest," explained Clayton as they reached the elevator and took it up two floors to his office. "But don't worry, Brett. All it really means is that I'm going to have to work a little harder and stay on my toes a little more. That's all. Don't worry about it. Honestly."

But Brett *did* worry about it. He remembered reading about Levy in *Time* magazine and *People* when he defended a guy who admitted raping a woman after breaking into her home. Due to a legal technicality, Levy got the man freed. Levy had defended his action on the grounds that if one person's rights are violated we, as a society, leave the door wide open to greater abuses leading right up to a police state. As far as Brett was concerned the "door" was wide open as it was, and that was the jail cell gate behind which criminals, including some of the most potentially dangerous, were supposed to be kept away from the public they had abused.

Brett arrived home about two in the afternoon after lunching with Clayton and read for approximately an hour, meditated, and made himself some dinner. He'd been lucky enough to locate an authentic Japanese grocery down on High Street near the capitol building. He and Kyoko used to go there every Saturday to shop for bamboo shoots, a rice he grew to like in Tokyo, and various Japanese herbs and spices difficult or impossible to find in standard grocery stores.

Brett enjoyed cooking and had become skillful in using the wok Kyoko had owned since she was a teen-ager. Brett used to cook at least twice a week. Kyoko had always welcomed the night off from the kitchen and Brett had really gotten into the joy of cooking.

And though the joy of living was gone for Brett now, he knew it would return. But tonight as he sliced the ginger and cleaned the shrimp and listened to Steely Dan's *Gaucho* on the stereo, something bothered him. It nagged at him. He felt an impediment had been thrown in the way of his road back to sanity.

About six o'clock Brett sat down in front of the TV with his shrimp, sauteed in ginger, and a glass of dry white wine to watch the news.

The lead story was Quentin Levy's press conference.

"I understand the grief, despair, and anger of this city," began Levy. "I understand, too, that there is a strong feeling that justice must be done. This, too, I understand. And it is to that very end that I have come to this great Midwestern city. In this country, the greatest possessions are those which cannot be held in one's hands. They are the rights of men everywhere. These guaranteed rights set us apart from barbarians, the Idi Amins of the world. The party or parties who have committed the heinous crimes against the fine family of this city should be dealt with harshly . . . but fairly. To sacrifice the rights of even the lowliest of criminals is to deal a mighty blow to the very heart of this country and to the free world everywhere.

"Thank you ladies and gentlemen."

The newscaster went on to summarize the case and theorize as to what consequences, if any, would be realized from the surprise entrance of Levy into the case.

After he finished dinner, Brett called Ted Clayton.

"Hi, Jenny. Is Ted there?"

"No. Brett?"

"Yes. Do you know where I can reach him?"

"I think he's down at the office."

"So late?"

"Something's up."

"With Levy?"

"Yeah. Call him down there. I'm sure you can reach him."

"Thanks," said Brett and hung up. He dialed Ted's office number.

"Ted?"

"Brett?"

"Yeah."

"Brett let me call you back."

"What the hell's going on?"

"Meet me at Sadie's about ten. I'll run it all down to you then."

"Trouble?"

"At ten," said Clayton and hung up.

This was it, thought Brett. That feeling he'd had. He'd known something was coming. The hours passed slowly and finally about nine-thirty Brett got into his Celica and drove into town to a small Italian restaurant near the capitol building.

There were just about six people in the bar. Brett ordered an Absolut vodka and waited for his friend.

Chapter 4

Clayton walked into the bar a defeated man and dumped himself sloppily into a chair opposite Brett.

"Son of a bitch," was all he said.

Brett took a deep breath and said, "What happened, Ted? Give me the stuff straight."

Ted waved at Barney behind the bar who already had the familiar lawyer's gin martini on the bar ready for the barmaid to deliver. She did and Ted took the whole thing in two swallows while the girl stood at the table. He raised one finger to indicate that another drink would be in order and finally looked Brett in the eye.

"We fucked up, Brett. Fucked up bad. I knew what had gone down and had hoped that some smooth-talker like Levy wouldn't get a crack at it. We tried to bury it, but that son-of-a-bitch found it."

"Found what?"

"Ah shit," muttered Clayton under his breath as the second martini was brought to the table. "Keep an eye on me, nurse," he told the girl. "I'm a sick man and I don't want my medicine to run out." She nodded and walked away.

"Everybody wanted these guys, Brett. Everybody wanted these guys bad. Too bad, as it turned out."

"What in the hell are you talking about?"

"Whoever nailed these guys was sure to land a promotion; no doubt about it. It was the biggest plum this department had to offer since the campus stranglings back in '47. Bigger than that or anything else around here *ever*, most would say. Anyhow, the two guys who actually tracked the trio down were, shall we say, a little overzealous. The dynamic duo thought they had a hot lead on some bikers and didn't bother getting the right judge to sign the search warrant to search the suspects' house. The house was located less than a mile outside the jurisdiction of the judge who signed it. The important word here, by the way, is 'outside.' All the evidence found in the house, as a result of an illegal search warrant, has got to be thrown out."

"But the confession?"

"They're saying that it was made under duress and, knowing Levy, he'll make a decent case that they were roughed up a bit."

"But there's other evidence."

"Not really. Everything that could definitely tie the suspects to the crime was in the house and everything in the house is now off limits. No one saw the suspects enter or leave your parents' house. No one can even confirm they were anywhere but where they now say they were—at home playing poker and drinking beer."

"So what does this mean, Ted?"

"I don't know, Brett. I just don't know."

"I think you do."

"Okay. We've still got a slight chance to get something on these guys, but it's a good bet that by now Levy has covered their tracks but good."

"The bottom line?"

"The fucking bottom line is that they're probably gonna walk."

"Even though everyone knows they butchered my wife and my parents," said Brett almost serenely.

"You got it."

"Is that justice, Ted? Is that the justice we talked about?"

"It's the same lady, Brett. But I'm afraid she's become a whore."

Both men finished their drinks in silence, then shook hands and embraced before parting company. Each had the feeling that he had left something behind that night, that somehow, just as surely as winter follows fall, a season had passed, a new time had begun. It was not a pleasant feeling.

It was a transitional season, like autumn, when one felt a greater presence of darkness than light and that things would become difficult before they would become easier, lighter again. Ted Clayton would never again lecture anyone on the merits of the justice system, to which he had dedicated his life. For him it was as if he had just discovered there was no Santa Claus, that all the faith he had acquired in the past was now scrapped, that the goddess, justice, for whom he toiled most of his life had been found to be a common tramp.

For Brett the break with a past, the recognition that he had changed, was no less marked. He hadn't changed with the subtlety and continuity of a bending branch, but rather he'd broken, cleanly, swiftly, irreparably. He was no longer the person he was before the break. He was someone else. And, like Ted, there was still some uncertainty as to what he had now become, what values he would now hold to be true.

Brett felt an ominous sense of purpose in his stride as he walked from the restaurant that night, as if he were headed somewhere with ferocious intent, but where that was he did not know. For the first time in his life he could sense something different in his consciousness. Though it was a new sensation, he knew what it was. He now had to understand it and learn to live with it before it destroyed him. For the first time in his life, Brett sensed violence strongly. Not just the sensation that it could happen *to* him. This was a sensation, a knowledge, that he could create that violence and that that violence could ultimately destroy the person he had become.

Snow flurries whirled in the cold night air as Brett walked down High Street toward the parking lot where he had left his car. He caught a reflection of himself in a shoe store window. He stopped and looked into the face of a violent man.

Chapter 5

The papers went wild the next day when the story was leaked and page after page read like an editorial against the justice system in America. One reporter was said to have a transcript of what the suspects had said when they were arrested. Although the paper didn't print the entire transcript, one excerpt particularly sickened Brett:

"We was just gonna rob the place, you know," said the suspect known as Eddy. *"We were cruisin' the rich folks' turf when we saw all these fancy cars and that, and, you know, we'd had a few beers. So anyhow, we parked the car a few blocks away and waited out back in the woods until everybody'd left. Yeah, like we only wanted to rob the place, but hell, we just got into the whole thing; I mean it was really fun. I mean violence is beautiful. People don't understand that, but that's their own thing. I dealt with that when I was a kid and my head is on straight about that. Hell, we was just gonna rob that place. Thing is, we was just having too damn much fun to stop. We just got carried away. No big deal or nothin', just got carried away."*

The article went on to say the suspects were found to be high on angel dust and were incoherent and violent during their arrest.

Levy arranged for the suspects' immediate release and the city became a media circus with Levy serving as ringmaster.

"Certainly, I have compassion for the surviving family

member," said Levy on an interview show the night the prisoners were released. "But I also have respect for the Constitution of the United States. These men's rights were trampled on in a fashion that would have made the Gestapo proud. We don't live in a fascist state, yet. And as long as there is breath left in this body, I will do everything in my power to fight injustice wherever I see it."

Brett turned the TV off and called Ted Clayton.

"How you doin', Brett?"

"Okay. Want a drink?"

"Sure. Same time, same place."

"See you about ten," said Brett and hung up.

The press had done their usual job of hounding the distraught by showing up the morning of the release and asking Brett such questions as, "How does it feel to know that the killers of your family have been set free?" and—a classic—"How do you feel about the former suspects in your family's slaying?"

Brett had said, "Same as you or anyone else would feel, asshole," and shut the door in their faces. Needless to say, Brett's comments had not made the evening news.

Brett found Ted Clayton sitting in one of the darker corners of Sadie's, nursing what didn't look to be his first drink of the evening. Brett sat down across the table from the lawyer, flagged down the waitress and ordered an Absolut.

"So, how are you doing?"

"Okay," said Clayton. "No, not really. Pretty piss poorly if you want to know the truth."

"It's all over then."

"Whenever P.T. Barnum decides to bring down the curtain. But yeah, it's over. And me, I'm looking in the want ads. Think I'm going to try and get a job selling hamburger, used cars, what the hell ever."

"You're taking this pretty hard."

"I loved your mom and dad, Brett. They were like my second parents. And I loved the law. Sure, I knew it had its problems, but not this bad. I just wasn't prepared for this. I feel so damned tired of it all now. My motivation is gone. I don't know exactly what I'm going to do now. I've thought about . . . I've been doing a lot of thinking."

"Me too."

"I'll bet," said Clayton, his eyes meaningfully riveted on Brett's. "That's not an alternative Brett, believe me."

"What are you talking about?"

"You know what the hell I'm talking about. And I'm telling you to . . . Oh hell, I'm not telling you anything anymore. I'm no goddamned sage."

An Absolut on ice was set in front of Brett and he sipped at it briefly before saying, "I appreciate what you did, Ted. You did all you could."

Ted started to say something, but stopped when he heard a commotion coming from the entrance of the restaurant. Both men turned to see what was going on. In walked Quentin Levy and a few men and women Brett recognized as reporters. They were given a table far away from Brett and Ted's table. But soon after they were seated, a waitress told the famous lawyer that Brett was in the bar and Levy ventured into the darker part of the establishment, entourage in tow.

"Brett Ashford?" said Levy amiably, extending his hand. Brett looked into Levy's eyes calmly, yet coldly, and let Levy's hand hang in the air like an offensive joke. Levy smiled and withdrew his hand.

"Son, I want you to know that there are no hard feelings."

Brett tried to steady himself. What he wanted to do would have left Levy in traction for months, or longer, but he replied simply, "Oh?"

"Brett," interrupted Clayton. "He's got the press right behind him and they're gonna write down everything you say. Be cautious. Better yet," said Clayton glaring right at Levy, "tell the son of a bitch to fuck off!"

"The retort of a learned counselor," said Levy to Clayton.

"Look," said Brett to Levy, "my wife, my mother and my father were hacked to death like turkeys for Thanksgiving. The guys who did it said they couldn't help themselves because they were having too much fun. You are responsible for making sure those members of society can continue to have *fun* when they are in the mood to do so. The next time they're in the mood for a party I hope to God they invite your wife and kids.

"Now get the fuck out of my sight before I make you send *me* to jail."

"Well, if that's the——"

"Stop. Just get out of my sight."

Levy coughed a little and walked away followed by the reporters who were considerably less jovial than when they had arrived at Brett's table.

"Let's get out of here," said Clayton. "One thing, though."

"Yeah?"

"You said it right, old man. You said it the way it should have been said. And I hope the papers write it down word for word, expletives and all."

"But they won't."

"No, they won't."

The two men finished their drinks, left the bar and walked toward a nearby parking lot where Brett had parked his car. Several people were walking toward the two and Brett recognized one of the men in the group as one of the suspects.

"Shit! Look Brett, let it ride," said Clayton when he recognized the man.

"It's cool," said Brett. "I'm not going to kill anybody . . . at least not in front of witnesses."

As the two groups came together, the suspect recognized Brett and stopped.

"Hey look," said the man to the others with him. "You know who that is? That's Brett Ashford. Hey man," he said extending his hand to Brett. "The whole thing was a mistake. Honest. We had nothing to do with it. Johnny was just talking out of his head about the stuff we was supposed to have done. We were just a little high, ya know?"

Brett stepped close to the man and a tension filled the air— the kind of tension created by a cold blade against sweating skin. Clayton thought about grabbing for Brett but knew that if Brett had decided to do something, there was nothing he could do now.

"Yeah?" said Brett simply.

The other man swallowed and fear danced in his eyes. "Yeah. Honest."

"And you'd tell me the truth, wouldn't you?"

"Sure man," said the other feeling only a little more confident.

Brett was standing nearly toe to toe with the suspect and he reached out and pointed to something on the man's shirt. "Gotta stain on your shirt."

The man looked down and as he did Brett brought his right index finger straight up against the man's nose.

"Owww!" screamed the man as much out of shock as pain. "What the fuck!"

"An old joke. Must have done it a little too hard," said Brett as a trickle of blood appeared just below the suspect's nose.

"Damn right!" said the man, his fear holding his reflexes in check.

Brett leaned over and whispered something into the man's ear and slapped him on the back and said, "See you around."

Then Brett motioned to Clayton and the two walked away from the stunned suspect and the others.

"What did you say to him?"

Brett looked at Clayton and smiled. "Is this privileged communication, counselor?"

"You know it."

"I told him I had just let him live. For now."

"What did you do?"

"An eighth of an inch one way or another, and he'd be a dead man."

Chapter 6

When Brett arrived home that night, he knew that a plan was formulating naturally in his head. He wasn't sure exactly what that plan was, but he felt that it was already in motion.

Brett's father had left everything to Brett's mother and to Brett, which meant that Brett now had become considerably wealthy. Brett informed his lawyer and accountant that he wanted all his father's properties liquidated as soon as possible and the money put in his own account. The process, which took about six months, made Brett a millionaire nearly twice over. Even after taxes and with the aid of a few well-paid, hotshot lawyers recommended by Clayton, Brett was able to keep more than half of it.

Slowly, quietly, the money began to disappear. Brett funneled it into accounts in foreign banks under a new name— Brett Wallace. He told no one and it was done in such a way as not to arouse suspicion.

Brett tied up all his father's outstanding business obligations and after about eleven months, the financial slate was nearly clean. But the emotional slate still needed to be erased.

"Long time no see, Brett," said Clayton sitting down across a table covered with a red-checkered cloth. Brett had already ordered drinks for them both and Clayton immediately started sipping his gin martini.

"About a month," said Brett.

"Jenny's always asking when you're coming back for her stuffed pork chops."

It had been nearly a year since the tragedy and neither man spoke of it now. It occasionally reappeared in looks and awkward moments when something would happen that reminded them of the killings. But, for the most part, it was a bad memory both men worked at keeping out of their relationship. Clayton tried even harder than Brett. For the lawyer the incident had been an abject failure, the low point in his career, his life. It had been a turning point. Shortly after the case was thrown out, Clayton quit his job as D.A. and returned to private practice. He cited personal reasons. The fact was, he no longer had the stomach for law; or at least the law the way it was practiced by such high-powered types as Quentin Levy. Returning to private practice gave Clayton more control over his work. Since then, he had been piecing his life back together, trying to replace the now-shattered constants with new ones.

He and Brett saw each other every few weeks or so, but he was not really aware of what Brett was doing, except that he knew he had liquidated his father's assets, which Clayton had strongly advised against. But he didn't push. He didn't feel much like giving Brett advice.

"Ted, I wanted us to get together tonight because I'm going away for a while."

"Oh? Where do millionaires go nowadays?" said Clayton kidding.

"I'm not sure. I'll just let my mood be my guide," said Brett. But there was no playfulness in his tone; it was not the tone of a man preparing for a pleasure cruise.

"Why now?"

"Everything's ready."

Clayton was beginning to get the feeling that there was something more to what Brett was saying.

"What's this all about?"

"I'm not sure I know what you mean."

Clayton thought a minute, scanned the events of the past several months, took a deep breath and let it out. He took a long pull on his martini before he spoke.

"You're not coming back, are you?"

"Probably not, Ted."

Clayton looked down at the table, then out the window, not knowing what to say. The two didn't say anything for a few moments. They both ordered linguine with white clam sauce and a bottle of good chablis.

"You haven't changed your mind from that night we talked in my den, have you?"

"No," said Brett, not volunteering any information.

The food and wine arrived and the two ate most of the meal in silence.

Finally Clayton said, "Brett, I can't help but feel that I failed you."

"Ted, *you* haven't failed me. The system failed me. It's failed us all."

"Are you sure you've thought this thing out?"

"Very carefully. It's something I have to do."

"You'll be the prime suspect; you know that."

"I'm not sure I know what you're talking about Ted, but if I did, I'd say that I think I've taken care of everything; at least, as much as can be anticipated."

Clayton raised his glass to make a toast. As he looked into Brett's eyes, Brett saw tears gathering in the lawyer's eyes. "Make those sons-of-bitches pay, Brett. Make them pay," said Clayton, his voice cracking at the end.

Brett said nothing, but simply raised his glass and touched it with Clayton's.

Chapter 7

The next day Brett made a call from a phone booth.

"Hello. Is this Johnny Howard?"

There was silence on the other end of the line. Then, "Who wants to know?"

"My name is Lester Graves, from Atlas Publishing in New York. You've heard of us, of course."

"Oh yeah, sure. I've seen your maps."

"We don't publish the maps. We're bigger than that company. Anyhow, I've been sent to Columbus to talk with you about getting your story about the Ashford killings."

"Hey man, we didn't do that. What kind of shit is this?"

"This is a serious offer, Mr. Howard. We're well aware of the legal ramifications. First of all, let me say that you and your associates, the other ex-suspects, would be paid in excess of one million dollars for your story."

"Wouldn't do us any good if we were in jail, would it."

"You wouldn't be in jail. The book would be a fictionalized account of what happened. According to our legal people, there is a way we can get around the whole thing and still play on the publicity of the trial."

"I don't know."

"Look, all I ask is that we get together and talk about this. After all, it's worth a million dollars or more to you and your friends."

"Okay, so what do we do? I'm not saying we're gonna do it or nothin', I just want to know what you propose."

"So that you are guaranteed privacy and so that you don't

think we're trying to set you up or record you, I've chosen a remote spot out in Grove City to meet. I understand from the locals that the place I have in mind would offer us the seclusion we require. You see, our company is not anxious to have the press see us together and be accused of . . . well, taking advantage of others' grief. You know what I mean."

"Yeah, sure. Hold on a minute."

Howard went off the line for a minute and then came back on. "Okay. But us meetin' you don't mean nothin', you know. It's just that we'd be stupid not to listen to somebody offerin' us a million bucks to make up stories. You know what I'm sayin'?"

"Certainly, Mr. Howard. I think you've made the right decision."

"So where do we meet you?"

"You know where Frank Road intersects with the Grove City Highway?"

"Yeah."

"Drive about five miles west on Grove City Highway toward Grove City and you'll come to a burned out grocery store. You'll see a sign still standing in front which reads 'Smith's Grocery.' Go about a half mile beyond that and you'll see a dirt road off to your left. It's not marked, but there's a large rock, a boulder, sitting next to the road. It's got a heart painted on it in blue and there are initials inside the heart. Turn onto that road, follow it into the woods and you'll eventually come to my car. I'll be driving a blue Ford."

"Okay. I got it. What time?"

"Tomorrow at two p.m. would be fine."

"Okay. Now you better be there or we'd be real upset, if you know what I mean. It's a long way for us to come. You just better be there."

"I've come a long way, too. I'll be there. See you there tomorrow at two," said Brett and hung up.

The sky was gray the next afternoon. The temperature was in the mid-forties. The ground was rock-hard and a chilly wind blew across the field into the woods. Brett felt cold and alone as he lay in wait behind a large tree stump about twenty-five yards from where his rented blue Ford was parked. This was the day he had both dreaded and looked forward to for almost a year. The men he now lay waiting to execute had brutally killed his family and now he would do the job the system had failed to do. It was a job that, not long ago, Brett had thought he would never have had the stomach for.

Preparation for today had been complete, or so Brett hoped. But no amount of preparation could completely prepare a man to kill another man. Still, Brett knew he was as ready as he would ever be.

It was now nearly two o'clock and three men on motorcycles would come into sight any minute. Brett knew they'd be on motorcycles today, although they sometimes took the one car they had between them. They'd been riding their cycles lately, Brett had observed, and, just to make certain, Brett had tampered with their car the night before. The car would not start today. The men usually rode their bikes no matter the temperature, as long as it wasn't snowing, but today Brett could leave nothing to chance. Everything was down to a schedule, a tight schedule; a schedule Brett had gone over and over in his mind so often that it was second nature to him now.

But the waiting, damn the waiting, thought Brett. He hated these men, but he'd never killed anyone before. He'd never harmed *anyone* before now.

To some, Brett knew, he would be labeled a psychopathic killer no better than the garbage he was disposing of. To others he would become a hero, a man who did a job society was too inept to do. But Brett knew he was neither a hero nor a villain. He was simply a human being who had been cruelly wounded and who felt a need for some balancing of the scales, thereby exorcizing the pain three men had caused him. In the beginning he had been content to play by society's rules. In fact, he would have preferred it that way. But those rules proved to be patently unfair to a point that no lucid argument could be made in their defense, only apologies.

But Brett had not been content with apologies. He wanted —he needed—justice. And, to him, in the end only one thing seemed fair.

In the distance Brett heard the sound of loud engines, the

thunder. It would roll closer and closer and Brett would deliver the lightning.

The men laughed and yelled to each other as they drove down the road toward the woods. Through the barren trees they could just make out the blue Ford and headed in that direction. They were bunched close together because the road was narrow. All three bikers simultaneously hit the branch covered ditch Brett had dug.

Brett raced to the scene and heard moaning, but all three men were conscious and moving. All were dazed so that when Brett reached into the tangled mess and dragged each man out, he experienced little resistance. Brett led the stunned trio into a clearing about twenty yards from the ditch. He waited a while before holding smelling salts under their noses until they could focus on him.

"Do you know who I am?" Brett said as the men began to come to.

The man to whom Brett had given a nose bleed said, "Yeah, *I* know who you are. You're Brett Ashford. Look man, you've got it all wrong. We didn't kill your parents *or* your wife."

"That's not what the papers said."

"They were wrong."

"I'm never going to rest until I've exterminated you scum," said Brett with feeling.

Brett noticed that one of the men—the one he recognized from the papers as the leader, Johnny Howard—was making a covert move just within the periphery of Brett's sight. He noticed a hand signal passed from Howard to the man on Brett's left, who started to grab for a knife in his boot. Brett moved for the man's boot and as he did Howard moved to grab Brett from behind. Brett put up a struggle, but finally Howard commanded a firm grip on him from behind and the two others threw a few punches that landed hard.

"Whatcha gotta say now, Ashford?" howled Howard in Brett's ear.

"What are you guys going to do?"

"Oh, I don't know. Do you play bridge?" said one of the other men. The bikers laughed while Brett struggled against Howard's grip.

"Tell me one thing," pleaded Brett. "For God's sake, please

tell me before you kill me if you killed my family. Don't let me go to the grave with that question unanswered. A last wish, please."

"Well Johnny, what do you think?" said one of the men.

"Oh hell, I think the guy's got a right to know," said Howard.

"You know, Ashford, I'd never had an Oriental girl before. And pregnant at that. When she started yelling that she was pregnant, boy that really turned me on."

"I had to be sure," said Brett, all his senses converging in a single whirlpool of rage. His entire body, all his limbs were on automatic, animated by a vengeance so terrible, so intense that Brett felt he might simply explode and kill them as though he were a human bomb.

But that wasn't the way it happened.

Brett stepped back with his right foot and brought it down with enough power to break nearly every bone in Howard's foot. Howard let go his bearhug on Brett and doubled over. As the biker's forehead began its downward descent, Brett's elbow came back into it with such force that it popped Howard's skull like a melon. Howard was dead before he hit the ground. The other two men stood paralyzed with fear.

Finally they both started to run. Brett dove at one man from behind and tackled him. This was the man who had talked about raping Kyoko. Brett grabbed him between the legs and dragged him by his testicles for a few feet along the ground. Then, with sharp blows to the thighs and upper arms, broke the man's arms and legs. Then Brett rolled him over and, applying his knee to the man's spine, broke his back.

Brett spun and rolled out of the way as he heard a sound behind him. A stick landed heavily on the broken back of the dead biker. It was a blow aimed at Brett by the remaining man.

The man withdrew a knife from his boot to try to protect himself, but he knew he was outclassed and that he was about to die. Brett approached the man calmly. As the man lunged at him, Brett grabbed the knife hand and snapped the man's wrist as though he were breaking a piece of peanut brittle.

"You shit!" cried the man. "You're as bad as we are. You shit, you broke my fucking hand!"

"Are you sorry for what you did?"

"I'm sorry I didn't take an extra turn with your slant-eyed whore, you fucking asshole!" said the man and spit in Brett's face.

Brett turned as if to walk away, then did a roundhouse kick, the impact of which squashed the man's head. The lifeless—now faceless—body fell to the ground in a contorted spasm and just lay there sending a river of blood running into another red river not far away.

Brett dragged the three bodies over to the ditch he had dug and threw them in on top of their motorcycles. Then he covered the ditch with branches and leaves.

Brett put up a makeshift fence composed of rocks and branches and left part of the hole open so that no one else would drive or stumble into the gruesome grave.

After checking the ditch once more and covering the major puddles of blood with leaves and dirt, Brett went to his car where he cleaned himself off, changed his bloody clothes and put them into a plastic bag in the trunk of his car.

Then he drove back to a small hotel he had checked into near the airport, which was about twenty miles from the scene of the slayings.

Brett showered, shaved, and changed into a suit and tie. His suitcase was already packed. He patted his coat pocket inside of which was a ticket for a six o'clock flight to Tokyo via New York.

He checked out of the hotel about four-thirty and went to his car, which he had parked next to a large blue container the hotel used for garbage. The receptacle was piled high with brown plastic bags full of rubbish. The same type of bag Brett had noticed that morning, and picked up on his way to the afternoon rendezvous with the three bikers. He put the bag from his trunk into the blue container. Brett dropped off his rented blue Ford at Hertz at the Columbus airport and checked in for his New York flight about forty-five minutes early. He went to the airport bar and ordered an Absolut on the rocks and tried not to think of himself as a murderer.

He had thought of everything, planned it out down to the last detail, but there was no way to anticipate how he would actually feel when it was over. Brett had hoped, in spite of the facts, that he might have been wrong and the three weren't really responsible. But he knew too much about the case from Clayton to hold out much hope of that. Still, Brett had to hear the words, the confession, from their lips. He had set himself up as judge, jury, and executioner. There was no margin, absolutely none, for error.

Brett knew that four men, not three, had died on a deserted country road in Grove City. Besides the bikers, Brett Ashford had ceased to exist. He was now and forever Brett Wallace. His passport, his many bankbooks, his driver's license, all identification, the ticket now in his breast pocket, declared him to be Brett Wallace.

His mother and father were dead. His wife was dead. Brett Ashford was dead.

As Brett sat and sipped his vodka, he pondered his next move. He was a man without a past. All he had was a great deal of money and a destination, a place he knew he would be welcome. An acquaintance had been contacted and plans made. At this moment, Brett felt almost indifferent as to what those plans were.

He *did* feel something, though. It was a coldness, a chill. He knew now what most people only theorize about. He knew he could kill. What he *didn't* know was whether he could now live. Or, more importantly, *why* he should live.

He finished his drink, left a bill sufficient to cover the tab and walked down the long corridor toward the gate, away from his home, his past, knowing that he could never return.

Chapter 8

When Brett arrived in Tokyo the sun was shining and it was midday. No matter what the country or its traditions, airports looked the same all over the world.

Brett checked his baggage through customs, past the first hurdle. At least customs had not been alerted to his arrival.

Brett went directly to the Currency Exchange window and changed a few thousand dollars into yen, making certain to get his "Record of Purchase of Foreign Means of Payment" certificate.

Brett had traveled light. He picked up his single suitcase and briefcase, headed for the taxi island and hailed a cab. The ride downtown was uneventful. He had the driver drop him at the Takanawa Prince Hotel, which was picturesquely located on the top of a breeze-swept hill in one of the better parts of town, only minutes from the Ginza district.

But Brett didn't appreciate the beauty of Tokyo as he had a couple of years earlier. He was deep in thought, confused, and wondering if life could be lived on the terms he had now constructed for himself.

The man Brett was to meet was to do so only when Brett had ascertained he wasn't being watched or pursued by authorities.

In his room, Brett undressed and collapsed for several hours on his bed.

When he awoke the nightmare was still alive. He showered, dressed and went out into the early evening and the Ginza district.

The Ginza, famous for its many massive department stores, thousands of little shops, restaurants, theaters, night-clubs, bars, and crowds of people, was easily the busiest shopping district in Tokyo. Brett made his way through the crowded streets to a Yakitori shop he'd often frequented. Amid the clouds of smoke rising from the charcoal grills, he purchased a skewer of the cooked chicken, passing up the cheap sake available at such places.

Brett wasn't very hungry and the appetizer satisfied his meager hunger. He went into a nearby Suntory Bar and ordered a Suntory vodka. He didn't like it as much as Absolut, but it did the trick. He sat down in a corner alone and fended off a couple of interested young Japanese girls who were eager to make his acquaintance. He was not in the mood.

About an hour and three drinks later, a fight broke out at a table next to Brett's. One drunken Englishman had taken exception to what a drunken Australian had said about the Queen and the match was on. The Australian knocked the Englishman onto Brett's table spilling his drink all over him. Brett looked shocked. He had been oblivious to the beginning of the fight, oblivious to anything but a bizarre slow-motion recall of a scene in a small town in the mid-western United States.

Both men looked at the American. Brett looked up at the men. He thought about killing them.

But he just got up and left.

The next morning Brett awoke after a fitful night's sleep which was the result of getting oriented to another time zone and from the waking nightmare which would not leave him alone. He dressed, had breakfast in his room, and, about ten o'clock, ventured out into the unseasonably cool temperature and took a taxi to the Imperial Palace.

A soft mantle of snow etched natural graffiti against the stone walls rising out of both sides of the moat encircling the Palace. The main entrance to Japan's largest castle was over the Nijubashi, or double bridge.

The giant structure was the residence of the Tokugawa Shogun administration for 265 years. The tallest building remaining of the Shogun's castle was forty-two feet high and known as "Fujimi Yagura" or "Mount Fuji viewing tower," because from the top floor Mount Fuji could be seen on clear days.

But today was not clear, nor was the Imperial Palace open to the public. Indeed it was only open on January 2nd and on the Emperor's birthday on April 29th.

But Brett wasn't walking across the Nijubashi as a tourist. He had a meeting with an old friend.

Brett was early. He leaned over the slightly snow-covered railing of the bridge and looked out upon the river flowing peacefully beneath him. Birds flew overhead and the paradox of his feelings filled his head. He felt far from home, yet returned somehow to a source of something familiar that he could not adequately describe. He felt like a killer, yet also like a warrior who had only done what a warrior must do.

The American's thoughts were interrupted by the soft sound of snow crunching underfoot. He looked up and saw his friend.

"Welcome," said Master Yamaguchi when he had reached Brett's side. Both men bowed slightly.

"You look greatly troubled, my good friend," said Yamaguchi.

"More than I have ever been in my life, master."

Brett explained to Yamaguchi what had taken place, the murder of his family and his subsequent revenge.

"And how does this make you feel, Brett-san?" asked the Oriental.

"I don't know."

"You are a wise man, Brett-san. You know that is not so."

"It is a more complex feeling than I have ever felt before. I have killed three men. I contemplated killing them, planned it. In the eyes of the American law, I am a murderer."

"Are you a murderer, Brett-san?" asked Yamaguchi as the two continued to talk amid the lightly falling white which now powdered their hair.

"No. I am not. But . . ."

"But what?" said Yamaguchi softly.

"It's just that my whole system of right and wrong is totally turned around."

"Maybe, maybe not, Brett-san. Are you a man of honor?"

Brett thought about the question for a time and said, "I'm not sure."

Yamaguchi smiled comfortingly at the young American. "You are a confused man today, Brett-san. Not the man I talked with a short time ago."

"That is true, master."

"Honorable men do honorable things. Dishonorable men do dishonorable things. Were the men who killed your parents honorable men?"

Without hesitation, Brett answered, "No."

"Were these men repentant of their dishonorable deeds?"

"No, master."

"Were you certain that these men did exactly what you say they did?"

"Yes."

"Then, Brett-san, you tell me what was the honorable thing for you to do. Think on this thing. And think too, that what may be right and honorable for you, may not be so for another."

They stood in silence for some time, then finally Brett looked the old man in the eye and smiled. "Master Yamaguchi, I *am* an honorable man."

Yamaguchi's eyes twinkled slightly. A smile appeared on his face. The old man said simply, "I could have told you that Brett-san."

The two men turned and walked away from the Palace, and across the bridge.

The next day Brett and Yamaguchi were traveling on the Shinkan-sen railway to Maibara—approximately a three-hour ride on the Bullet Express. The seats were much like reclining airplane types. The panoramic view at one point included Mount Fuji.

Brett brought only a duffel bag full of toiletries and a change of clothing. There wasn't room for much luggage on the train, and he wouldn't be needing much of anything else where he was going. Whatever else he might require would be provided at his destination.

Brett and Yamaguchi stopped in Maibara for a meal, then took a late afternoon train, offering somewhat lesser accommodations and speed, for a two-and-a-half-hour ride to Kanazawa.

Located on the Hokuriku (Japan Sea Coast), Kanazawa was not a tourist spot. The city was about 350 years old. Samurai warrior houses still stood preserved as reminders of a glorious past. Castle-type walls lined the streets and, in many cases dead-ended many streets creating a sort of giant maze. In the old days this was considered desirable because strangers and enemies would become disoriented and lost.

Yamaguchi and Brett were met at the train depot by a Japanese introduced by Yamaguchi as Master Torii. Master Torii looked to be in his late forties, and extremely fit. His body was well-toned from what Brett could tell and his eyes shone with an almost fierce beam of will. He bowed and accorded his guests the usual courtesies of the country.

Brett and Yamaguchi were led by Master Torii to his house which turned out to be what Brett considered a small castle. It was four stories high, the length and width being approximately thirty yards square.

Greeted at the door by two men who bowed to Master Torii, the host then led his guests to the second floor and a private room, where sake was served by an Oriental woman, who left immediately.

"Does he know where he is?" Torii asked Yamaguchi in Japanese. Brett understood Japanese well enough to carry on a relatively uncomplicated conversation.

"I have not told him," said Yamaguchi. "But I believe he knows."

"Do you?" Torii asked Brett.

"I am at the home of a Ninja," said Brett.

"That is correct. And you wish to join us? Is that not so?"

"That is so," said Brett.

"Master Yamaguchi does not bring students here who are not ready to take this step. Therefore, your technical expertise is not in doubt. But that is a small part of being a Ninja. Your mind must be set to this, and to this alone. There is no room for doubt once the first step upon this path is taken."

"I understand," said Brett. "I was not ready until yesterday. But I am ready now."

"I can see it in your eyes," said Torii.

"I can see it in your eyes, too," said Brett.

The men drank sake together and gradually a glowing feeling came upon them; the feeling one would have at the reunion of old friends.

The life-style was spartan. Brett had a room to himself and he talked little with other Ninjas training in Kanazawa. The training was often more mental than physical and slowly Brett began to sense a kind of peace and inner strength that had only been hinted at in his previous meditation. He concentrated deeply and came into balance mentally, physically, and spiritually. Within a year he was more at peace than he had ever thought a man could be.

At the same time he was learning to become one of the most skilled and fearsome warriors on Earth. He was taught the healing arts of acupuncture and acupressure as well as their dark sides: using these energy points to kill. He studied the specialty of herbs and learned to make antidotes as well as poison. He learned to take pain and to administer it. He learned to jump as though he were on a trampoline. He learned to fall from three stories up and walk away unhurt. He learned what some would call magic. He learned, in some cases, to extend his energy field beyond the physical limitations of his body and interact with physical matter.

And he learned to be alone. And silent. He learned not to fear. For fear, he found, was an absolute waste of attention and energy which would be needed in time of conflict.

But all this took time, a great deal of time, not only to learn, but to perfect. Nine years passed before Brett knew he was ready.

"I guess you know it's time," said Yamaguchi to Brett one day.

Yamaguchi visited Kanazawa twice a year and whenever he did, he and Brett would spend hours walking and talking together.

"Yes master, I know."

"Where will you go, Brett-san?"

"San Francisco," said Brett with certainty.

"We have contacts there. When you leave I will give you several names and addresses of our people. What will you do?"

"I've given this a great deal of thought and I will offer my services to those who are terrorized, brutalized by others and have no one to turn to. I'm certain authorities have long given up hope of finding Brett *Ashford*. I'll set up a business in San Francisco and operate out of there. First, I'll quietly retrieve the money I deposited in accounts throughout the world. Therefore, money will be no problem. So I can dedicate myself totally to this service."

Yamaguchi did not ask Brett whether he was ready or not. He could see it in his eyes.

Brett Wallace was ready.

Chapter 9

In a tiny restaurant on Clement in the new Japan-town district of San Francisco, Brett Wallace finished his sashimi, chicken teriyaki and sake. He had never been to San Francisco before and his first few weeks there had been a process of orientation not only to West Coast life-styles, but to American life-style once again. He didn't worry about being recognized. All of his adult life prior to his trip to Japan to study with the Ninja he had a moustache and longer hair, and was slightly heavier than he was now. Now he was lean, clean shaven and his hair was trimmed stylishly short.

The waitress, dressed in a kimono, shuffled to his table and asked if he was finished.

"Yes. And could you ask the cook if he or she makes Unagi Donburi?"

"That is an unusual dish. It is not on the menu."

"I know, but I like this place so much, and I'd like to come back for a special meal. Money is no object," he said laying a fifty-dollar bill on the table to cover his check which came to less than ten dollars. "Please ask her."

The girl smiled, bowed politely, turned and went back to the kitchen. A couple of minutes later she returned and said, "Our cook, Rhea, said that your request is an unusual one, but that she would be willing to consider making a special dinner for you and your party. But special arrangements would have to be worked out with the management. She said she would be willing to talk with you about it if you would care to leave a number where she can contact you."

"What time do you close?"

"In half an hour."

"I'm going to be at a friend's apartment nearby," said Brett withdrawing a piece of paper and a pen from his breast coat pocket. "Have her call me at this number when she gets off work." Brett handed the waitress the card and left her a generous tip.

He left the restaurant, went across the street to a bar and ordered an Absolut. Then he just waited.

In about thirty minutes, the phone on the bar wall rang and Brett answered it.

"Hello," he said.

"Is this Mr. Wallace?" asked a female voice.

"Yes."

"This is Rhea, the cook from the restaurant you ate at tonight."

"Oh yes. I loved your cooking. You see, I've just come from Tokyo and I have a sophisticated palate for Japanese cuisine. And I must say, your dishes are by far the best I've tasted here in the States."

"Thank you. You are too kind."

"I would like to discuss a business proposition with you."

"I will listen."

"Can you meet me tonight?"

"Yes."

"Clancy's Bar and Grill, down on Union in about half an hour?"

"I'll take a taxi and meet you there."

"See you then."

Clancy's was going strong for a Wednesday night and Brett ordered a beer and stood at the bar and waited. It was a fashionably jeaned crowd and the livestock auctions were in full swing. But Brett wasn't interested, even though he was being viewed as a hot item by a peppery duo who looked as though they could add spice to anyone's life.

By the time he was about three-quarters through the beer, he saw her.

Even in the confusion of a crowded bar, the couple's eyes locked immediately. Rhea stopped when she saw Brett and it was a moment before she moved toward him.

"Rhea," said Brett when she had arrived at his side. It was

not a question. Though they had never met, they *knew* each other.

"Brett," she said.

"Follow me," he said and slid the last quarter of his beer across the bar on top of a five-dollar bill.

The two moved through the crowd and out the back door where a limousine was waiting. Brett opened the door for Rhea, and they both got in. Brett tapped the window twice, waited, then tapped it another time. The chauffeur slipped the car into gear and they were off.

"A signal?"

"I don't take chances. I'd never seen you before. I might have been tricked."

"Do you think you've been tricked?"

"Enchanted, yes. Tricked no."

Brett had been told certain things about Rhea, including the fact that she was attractive. But she was *stunning.* Physical beauty, which Rhea had, could only go so far. It was an indefinable quality that animated the features, composed them into certain postures, moved the limbs in graceful motion, that made Rhea so strikingly beautiful to Brett.

Yamaguchi had instructed Brett to make contact with Rhea by asking for Unagi Donburi, broiled eel with rice.

Her uncle had been a Ninja and her mother and father had been sympathetic and helpful to the Ninja many times. In fact, it was as a direct result of Rhea's father helping the Ninja that he had met his death. Her mother had died shortly after that of cancer. Rhea had been on her own since she was sixteen and now supported herself as a cook in the restaurant.

As they drove across the Golden Gate Bridge Brett took in the vision of womanhood sitting next to him, illuminated by the bridge's lights.

She wore a black skirt tastefully slit up one side to just above the knee, black high-heel shoes, a beige satin blouse over unfettered ample breasts which jutted out to form sensuous points in the smooth material.

Her black hair was straight and fell silkily over her shoulders down to the middle of her back. Her face was pale, but exquisitely featured and her thin red lips seemed to sparkle moistly whenever a street light caught them. But it was her eyes that did the damage, that made her the beauty she was. They were dark brown and deep. Brett could see in her eyes doorways to worlds of pleasure. When she looked at him, an electric communication sparked between them.

They drove through the quiet and nearly deserted streets of Mill Valley, up into the hills and stopped in front of a house. The chauffeur got out and opened the door for the couple. Brett said something to him and he drove away.

Inside, Brett led Rhea upstairs and turned on some lights to reveal a sumptuous living room with furnishings in natural colors. A bar stood in one corner. But the most striking feature of the house was the view. Brett led Rhea out onto the deck and they both stood out looking across the bay to where the San Francisco skyline was just beginning to disappear under a heavy fog.

"Can I get you a drink?"

"Some wine, perhaps. White."

"Your wish," said Brett and went to open a bottle of wine he'd picked up at an exclusive wine shop he had discovered earlier in the day.

He returned and handed Rhea a glass. "To you," he said. "The second most beautiful woman I've ever seen."

Rhea blushed slightly and the two touched glasses.

"Delicious," said Rhea.

"Yamaguchi sends his greetings to you and thanks you in advance for helping me. Here's a letter he gave me for you," said Brett withdrawing an envelope from his pocket.

"Thank you," said Rhea taking the envelope and setting it next to her purse. "I'll look at it later."

"You really are lovely, Rhea. I must admit I wasn't prepared."

She looked away, moved toward the railing and sipped at her drink. "But I was prepared for you."

"Oh?"

"A messenger arrived several weeks ago and said you would be coming. I was told a great deal about you. What you plan to do, your reputation as one of the most skillful Ninja in all Japan."

"You sound as if you don't approve."

"I neither approve nor disapprove. And I'm certain it makes no difference to you either way."

Brett just smiled.

"My uncle died as a Ninja and my father died helping my uncle. I understand that they died honorably. But still, I wish my father had lived longer. I hardly knew him. Therefore, I have mixed emotions about the Ninja. There is great danger in being a Ninja."

"I can take care of myself."

"I don't mean the physical dangers. You have set yourself up as an executioner, in some cases. Most human beings are not equal to that task emotionally or spiritually."

"I know what you're saying and when I first went to see Master Yamaguchi, I was not equal to it. I'd been hurt deeply. I was wounded and I reacted brutally and emotionally. But that was nine years ago. I'm ready now. I'm certain of it, and I know Master Yamaguchi is sure I'm ready."

"How do you know that?"

"He would have killed me rather than be responsible for setting a murderer loose upon the world."

Rhea sipped at her wine. "That is so."

"Rhea, I want to be totally honest with you," said Brett moving next to her. She turned and faced him.

"Please."

"The primary reason Yamaguchi took me in was not because I was a highly skilled martial artist, even though I was. There was another reason, a reason that goes beyond what most Westerners consider to be possible. Yamaguchi and I were friends. We shared a profound mutual bond, though we'd met each other only once before and had talked for only a few hours. Do you know what I'm getting at?"

"I believe so."

"I sense that with you, Rhea. You and I are old friends. I felt it the moment you walked into Clancy's tonight. I'd never laid eyes on you before, yet it was as though an old friend had returned from a very long journey."

"I sensed that, too. I feel it now." She set down her drink and looked deeply into Brett's eyes, into his soul. He took her hand in his and the world seemed to melt away into rivers of passion. Waves of emotion, yearning, pain and love washed across them both. They were there, and they were not.

Finally Brett took Rhea in his arms and held her tightly, pressing her breasts to his chest. He took her face in his hands and guided her lips to his and found her mouth deep and inviting. He took her by the hand and led her into the bedroom, two walls of which were windows facing out upon the bay and the city.

They both stood silently facing each other, her arms entwined around his neck, his hands resting gently on her buttocks. The light of the full moon shone dreamlike across the water and into the room. Brett unbuttoned the satin blouse to reveal two full, round breasts, slightly larger than most Oriental bosoms he had seen. The nipples jutted out expectantly. He slid the garment from her shoulders, then unzipped her skirt and let it fall to her ankles. She stood in panty hose, under which she was nude, and high heels. He caressed her enclosed cheeks, then slipped his thumbs inside the waistband of her panty hose and slowly peeled them down to her knees. Then, in one smooth motion, he brought both hands gently up her thighs to the warm, moist place where they converged. A whispered moan escaped from Rhea's mouth and she swallowed hard. Brett began to rhythmically massage her clitoris with the middle finger of his right hand while his left hand rose to cup her right breast. He licked the fingers of his left hand and began to roll her nipples between his moistened fingers.

Then Brett guided her down onto the bed and finished undressing her. He stood over her and undressed himself revealing his readiness to make love with her. He lowered himself onto her, lifting her legs so that they rested over his shoulders. He entered her gently and they united in spasms of ecstasy for the better part of the night.

Chapter 10

"Nice view," said Rhea, sipping her tea.

"I particularly like to take my morning coffee out here on the deck. Invariably San Francisco is buried beneath the fog, but I know it's there and every morning it appears magically like some Disneyland. Often by the time I get to the sports section."

Neither said much for a while. They just watched the fog, and a few sailboats making their way out into the bay. Brett sipped at his coffee which he had freshly ground this morning and put his hand on Rhea's.

"Last night was . . . well, it was . . ."

"Wonderful?" asked Brett.

She smiled. "That's the word, but it sounds so clichéd."

"What happened last night between us was anything but clichéd."

She leaned over the side of her chair and kissed him on the cheek. He turned slightly and kissed her firmly on the mouth.

"What now?" Rhea said, settling back and resting the tea cup and saucer in her lap.

"I expect we'll get married—certainly before lunch. Then I'll pick up the station wagon and the dog and you can go pick up some kids and I'll meet you back here for supper."

She laughed a little at his jesting. "You know what I mean."

"Yes, I know what you mean. But that's about the closest I can come to predicting an answer."

"I see."

"Look," said Brett taking her hand in his and looking her in the eye. "What happened last night was the most special exchange of feelings and emotions that's taken place in my life for ten years. But I've changed a lot in ten years. I was sure as hell not expecting to meet someone like you. Not now."

"Sorry," she said, a little sarcastically.

"C'mon, you're better than that. Look, you know what I'm doing here. I've got to get that part of my life squared away first."

"Tell me about it—what you have to get squared away."

"All right."

Brett told her about meeting Kyoko in Japan, about coming back to Columbus, about the killing of his family, the trial, the executions, and about his nine years training with the Ninja.

"So that brings me up to last night. I contacted you because Yamaguchi said you could be trusted, that you were capable, intelligent and would be willing to help whenever you could."

"Help you to do what?"

"I'm not the only one in this world who's been screwed over royally and had no recourse but to either take matters into his own hands or curl up and die. But unlike most people, I had the skills to do something about it. I plan to keep an eye out for people in trouble. Bad trouble. I'm looking for people who've exhausted every legal avenue, who simply have no other way out. I'll go to them unannounced, and do what I can to balance the scales. And the only payment I ask of those I help is that they not reveal my identity. Because if I become known, I'm finished. First, I'm wanted for the killings in Ohio. Second, there will probably be other murders along the way. Third, I would be hounded by anyone with a two-bit grudge against somebody else."

"So how will you find your clients?"

"Newspapers are full of sad stories. Television, radio, magazines, word of mouth. I'm sure I'll have plenty to choose from."

"Have you taken on any cases yet?"

Brett sipped the last of his now cool coffee. "No."

"That sounds like a qualified no."

"You should be a lawyer. You're perceptive, you know that?"

"Perceptive enough to realize you still didn't answer my question."

"Yeah, well, I *have* got something. I think."

"Can you tell me what it is?"

"I can."

"Will you?"

"Over lunch. Maybe."

"How about for sure."

"Over lunch."

Brett tossed the china into the dishwasher, and changed into a pair of jeans and a dark blue T-shirt that had a picture of two slim naked female legs in high heels on the front. His body, tanned and muscular, though more toned than bulging, tapered at the waist, and his small hips looked good in jeans. All this was not wasted on Rhea.

The couple drove back across the Golden Gate to Rhea's apartment on 29th. She changed into shorts, cut high to accent her firm sleek thighs, a pink T-shirt and tennis shoes.

Brett put the top down on his 450SL and the wind tossed their hair as they drove back across the Golden Gate and through Muir Woods.

"Where we going?"

"To one of my favorite spots for lunch."

As they drove up into the mountains, civilization fell behind them like a discarded garment. The city became smaller and smaller the more they climbed until finally it seemed to be a toy.

When they reached the top of Mount Tamalpais, Brett parked the car and said, "What do you think?"

"Some restaurant!"

"I thought you'd like it."

"Think we can get a table?"

"I know the maitre d'. How about an entire hillside?"

"Sounds good to me. But where's the food?"

Brett got out of the car, went around to the trunk, opened it, and withdrew a picnic basket.

Rhea smiled. "How sweet. But when—"

"While you were getting dressed this morning at my place I just threw together a few things."

Brett took Rhea by the hand and led her down a narrow dirt path about a quarter of a mile to a grassy cliff which jutted out like an arrow and faced toward Sausalito, Mill Valley, and beyond to where the San Francisco skyline, now out of fog, glistened like some tiny jeweled music box in the distance.

"This is beautiful," she said.

"It's far from the restrooms, but it has its charm."

"It's very romantic, too."

Brett just smiled. "Got an appetite?"

"What did you bring?"

Brett opened the basket and withdrew a champagne bottle chilled in ice packed inside a small bucket. "A good year. I think you'll approve," he said playfully. Then he removed a plastic container full of sliced meats. "From Scarantino's. I've made friends with the owner. These are the best cuts. And fresh. I picked them up just before I had supper at the restaurant last night. Some bread," he said pointing to a loaf of French bread, "grapes, a mango, and a sizable chunk of Swiss cheese."

"And where are the napkins?"

"Here," he said taking out two cloth napkins in round holders from the basket.

"This is lovely, Brett. Really lovely." She moved close to him and kissed him slowly, sensuously on the mouth.

With one hand Brett slipped the champagne back into the cold pack and put his other hand around Rhea's waist. He bent her back until she was lying prone and he snuggled in beside her. He raised her T-shirt so that one breast was showing and he bent to kiss it.

"Brett, we're outdoors!"

"Yamaguchi told me you were quick."

"You know what I mean."

"I like to make love outside. Besides, no one can see us up here anyway. And if they try that hard to be voyeurs, they're entitled to a reward."

"But Brett," she began, and stopped as he kissed a

little harder on her other nipple. He slid his mouth down to her stomach and then pulled her shorts down and they made love on the soft grass.

When they were finished and dressed Brett asked, "So, what do you think about making love outside?"

She smiled. "I like it."

"Thought you would. We'll have to do it again sometime."

"Yes. There's something different about making love in such a large space. People are so used to making love in dark places where you feel no sense of space or in cars or small rooms. But outside with birds flying overhead, where you can see and feel nature for miles in every direction, well, it's just such a unique feeling of freedom."

"You're just an exhibitionist."

"You're terrible."

"How about some lunch? I've got quite an appetite now."

"Me too."

Brett set out the food and the two lovers enjoyed one of the best lunches either could remember.

"Rhea, I've got a proposition for you."

"I think I've already heard it."

"I mean a business proposition."

"Oh?"

"Even though I've got a decent amount of money, I've got to use that money to make more money so I don't arouse suspicion about myself. In other words I've got to go into business."

"And?"

"And I'd like you to run that business for me. I want to open a restaurant. We'd be partners. I'll put up the money and you run the place. We'd split fifty-fifty."

"I'd have to think about it."

"How long?"

"About two seconds."

"I'm not sure I can wait that long."

"Sure. I accept your offer."

"Let's make it the best Japanese restaurant in all of San Francisco."

"Japanese? I wanted to do an Armenian restaurant," said Rhea playfully.

"Anyhow," said Brett ignoring her comment, "we'll do it up right. The proper, tasteful atmosphere; the right ads in the right places; the right critics invited. How about that. The best restaurant in town—you really are a fabulous cook—and I'll have an explanation for living the good life in Marin County."

They toasted the deal with some champagne and lay back together, her head on his shoulder.

"You come up here often?"

"When I need to center myself."

"For a case?"

Brett didn't say anything. He sat up and wrapped his arms around his drawn up knees, rested his chin on his knees, and stared out into the distance.

"You told me you'd tell me about it over lunch," said Rhea.

"I told you I might."

There was total silence for a time. Rhea patiently waited for Brett to make up his own mind.

"Yes. For a case."

"You've decided on your first case?"

"Yes."

Again there was an extended silence.

"I've been following a series of incidents down in Los Angeles. Some old people are being terrorized by a gang. It started when one of the old people testified against two of the gang members about six months ago. His testimony sent one guy to a juvenile facility for a couple months, and the other guy to jail for a couple of years. The retribution started with petty harassment. But it escalated into purse snatchings, beatings, burglaries, and so on. And none of the old people want to risk filing a complaint because they're afraid they'll get beaten up or worse."

"What about the police?"

"They can only do so much. These gang members aren't stupid enough to commit a crime with a cop standing around. Therefore, somebody's got to report the crime and file a complaint. And that is exactly what cannot be done."

"Then how does anyone even know these things are going on?"

"The L.A. Times sent an undercover reporter into the neighborhood—an older guy—somebody who could get close to what was going on—and he came back with the story."

"What are you going to do? Go in like the Lone Ranger and clean house?"

"No. I've got to go in unnoticed and come out the same way. Except for one thing."

"Which is?"

"The trouble will be over."

"And how do you do that?"

"My way," said Brett simply. But there was something in the way he said it that couldn't have been made more potent had he yelled it from the top of his lungs and made it echo through the Grand Canyon.

They were both silent for a while as the unasked questions sounded in their minds. There would be violence. This was Brett's first case and he would not know what he was getting into. And Rhea had been through this before with her uncle and with her father. There was a good chance that someone would die. The Ninja code of honor would not allow Brett to back off from his stated goal. Either the gang would understand and stop, or one or all of them would die. Or, she thought, Brett would die.

Rhea made a small, forced smile and put her head on Brett's lap.

"So when are you going?"

"Soon."

"What about our restaurant?"

"My lawyer knows what I intended to do about that. Meeting you was just a formality. I'll call him when I get home tonight and he'll have the papers drawn up and sent to you. I've even got a location picked out."

"Let's go there. Tonight. For dinner."

"But it's just a few empty rooms. The kitchen equipment isn't even all in yet."

"Can you get the keys?"

"Sure, the guy who owns the place lives across the street from the spot, but——"

"Come on, Brett," she said stroking the inside of his right thigh.

He heaved a deep sigh of surrender and said, "Okay."

"Dinner at eight then?"

"I'll pick you up at seven forty-five."

The couple stayed on top of the mountain for a while longer. The Pacific Ocean was now coming into view through a light mist off to their right. They didn't say much. But then they didn't have to. They were old friends.

Brett called his lawyer when he got home and made the last minute arrangements regarding the restaurant contracts and told him that he would be leaving town for a few weeks and would call him when he returned. The restaurant was to be a number one priority while he was gone. Brett could give orders like that to the attorney he was paying well and expect them to be followed.

Brett settled back in his favorite chair and watched a blanket of fog settle in over the city. The lights on the sailboats came on and glided across the bay. He appreciated his life in Mill Valley and there were times he felt he'd paid enough dues for a lifetime, that maybe he should just kick back and enjoy what he had. But then it would come back to him——a feeling that a person had when he recognized his life had purpose. Brett's life had a purpose and it was not to retire from the human race. In a simplistic sense it seemed to Brett that somewhere along the line the bad guys had begun to outnumber the good guys. He wasn't sure how it had happened, though he had a few ideas.

People were being terrorized, dreams and lives shattered violently. And no one was coming to the aid of the victims. Authorities stood in line to help the criminal, but the victim needed somebody to plead his case. And, unfortunately, the only eloquence that was understood by most criminals was the language of violence. Brett did not consider himself a violent man, but if somebody slaps one's face and one cannot reason with the perpetrator, there are only two alternatives: learn to enjoy the pain or hit him back.

Strangely, society had created a majority of people who were unwilling to fight back because they were taught that those who violated the rules of society would be dealt with accordingly, or, who *couldn't* fight back.

But Brett *could* fight back and he *would* fight for what he believed in. And society—which he had championed, despite its faults—would get his complete aid. He'd be damned if he'd see it spat upon and destroyed by punks and hoodlums. He'd be damned if he'd just look on while the rights and possessions of the working man, the man who paid the bills, were trampled on and taken from him.

Responsible people used their talents and assets to the betterment of the world in which they lived, for the betterment of their fellowmen. Brett had talents and assets unlike any person he knew and he planned to use them the way he saw fit.

Brett's phone rang. "Hello."

"Brett, this is Rhea."

"Hi."

"I wonder if you would do me a favor?"

"Just about anything."

"You know the number of the guy who has the key to the building where the restaurant's going to be?"

"Yes."

"Could you call him and ask him if I can pick it up?"

"Sure. But why?"

"I'm going to get there a little before you do. I've got an idea."

"But it's not cleaned up or . . ."

"Hey, I know that. Just let me, okay?"

"All right. I'll call him. The address is 4118 Clement between 23rd and 24th. Only about eight blocks from you, as a matter of fact. The guy with the key is directly across the street at 4121 Clement. He's always there. I'll call him and tell him you'll be by."

"Great. So I'll put you down for an eight o'clock reservation, Mr. Wallace. That's a party of two?"

"That's right. See you then," said Brett and hung up. Rhea was a good woman. He was glad, very glad, he'd met her.

Brett found a parking place around the corner from the unfinished restaurant, went to the locked door and knocked. No answer. He knocked again. The door opened.

"Wallace. Party of two," he said.

"Come in. I'll see if your table is ready."

Brett walked in and a table with a candle burning brightly on it stood in the center of the room.

"Your table, sir," said Rhea leading him to his seat.

He smiled. "This is delightful, Rhea. You didn't have to bring candles, the electricity works."

"I know."

"How did you cook the food?"

"I made it all at home and brought it over with me."

Brett took in the surroundings, which Rhea had cleaned up. He took in the romantic ambience: the table, the checkered cloth, the candle. He took in Rhea's beauty. She was dressed in a black skirt, attractively slit up one side just above her knee, and a white silk blouse under which she obviously wore no bra. Her long black hair glistened in the candlelight and a sultry flame burned in her eyes.

"You look—Rhea you look beautiful."

"For a knight in shining armor, a girl has got to look her best."

Rhea produced a small thermos from under the table, removed the top and poured them each some sake.

"You think of everything," he said.

She smiled and put the thermos back under the table.

"To you," he said.

They both drank from tiny sake cups Rhea had brought.

"A special occasion?" asked Brett.

"You're going away soon. Right?"

He just said, "Yes."

"So this is your going-away supper. For good luck. With the restaurant and with . . . your business."

The supper was excellent. Brett knew he'd made the right choice asking her to run the restaurant. After they'd finished eating, Brett took the tablecloth from the table, put it on the floor and the couple made love upon it.

Brett knew he'd made the right choice with her as a lover, too. But they didn't discuss what that meant. They both knew there were no answers. He might come back, he might not.

And the scenario would be repeated over and over again. Neither wanted to burden the other with commitments. It wouldn't be fair to either party. So they made love as if there were no tomorrow. Because, for them, that was always a distinct possibility.

Chapter 11

Los Angeles and San Francisco were both on the West Coast and both in the same state, but beyond that they didn't have much in common.

Brett rented a car at L.A. Airport under the name B. Alexander and drove into L.A. to the Wilshire district. He spent the afternoon looking for an apartment from which to operate. Finally, he located one on Cloverdale. It was carpeted, furnished and had all the charm of a rubber glove. But people obviously seemed to go for that type of thing, because Brett rented the only vacancy.

The roof housed a Jacuzzi and a sauna and from it one could see, smog permitting, the downtown skyline. The roof was covered with artificial green grass, the kind you vacuumed instead of mowed. Standing next to the bubbling Jacuzzi, Brett felt a great sense of homesickness.

The next morning Brett went for a walk and tried to acclimate himself to Southern California. He noticed he coughed a little and his eyes burned, but the smog didn't seem to bother anyone else. He guessed he'd get used to it.

He went to the newsstand and picked up a copy of the L.A. Times and perused it over coffee at a local doughnut shop. Nothing on the Wilshire district case.

He found a local weekly and read it. The front page story was about what residents could do to protect themselves. Although it referred to specific gang threats and deeds only obliquely, the article reflected public fear.

"This business is awful," he said to the middle-aged woman behind the counter.

"What's that?" she said.

"This," he said tapping the local paper's headline: "We Must Protect Ourselves!"

"Yeah, sure is. I tell ya, I've lived around here most of my life. Grew up a few blocks away, as a matter of fact. Never seen nothin' like this before. Crime, sure. This is the big city. But nothin' like this."

"What makes this so different?"

"Not a day goes by, somebody doesn't come in here with a horror story. Cops can't do nothin'. Old ladies gettin' raped, old men gettin' beat up. In broad daylight, no less. Businesses around here are sufferin' as much as the old folks; well, maybe not *that* much. But it's bad. Real bad."

"So what are people doing about it?"

"Some move. After spending their whole lives here. Don't seem right, some punks come in here and run good people out of their homes. Some just stay inside all the time. Have groceries delivered; just stay inside, watch TV and jump every time they hear a noise. Just ain't right. And that's the truth."

"What about you?"

"They know better than to come after me. I'd kick 'em where it hurts. They'll only pick on people who don't offer no resistance. Hey, I haven't seen you around here before."

"Just moved here. I'm from Indiana. Not much crime there. Not yet at least."

"Not much action either, though," she said laughing a little.

"You'd be surprised."

"So what brings you out to the good life?"

"Company transferred me. I'm in the rubber business. Tires, balls, you know."

"You got a place around here?"

"Yeah, just a few blocks away. Didn't know I moved into a war zone, though."

"Hell, they'll leave you alone. You look like you could throw a punch."

"I keep in shape." Brett sipped his coffee, then asked, "Who are these kids anyhow?"

78

"Hell, I don't know. You hear all kinds of things. Makes 'em sound like Al Capone's gang, except ten times more cruel. One of the problems is people just don't know what to believe. I mean things happen, sure, but people are so scared that for every *one* thing that really happens, people make up three more horror stories."

"So what do I owe ya?" He wiped his mouth. The paper napkin was decorated with a doughnut with a smiling face.

"That'll be ninety-seven cents."

Brett handed her two dollars, thanked her for the chat and promised to come back soon.

As he walked back to his apartment he could sense, even smell, the fear in the air. Merchants sat lazily behind their counters. Some had even brought in television sets to pass the time. Theirs was a business that catered to the elderly, the walk-ins from the area. The neighborhood seemed to Brett like a doctor's waiting room full of patients sitting around waiting for bad news.

Inside his apartment building, Brett stopped by the group of mailboxes and noticed his name had been put up already. While he was checking that out, someone was checking him out.

"You B. Alexander?" a voice asked.

Brett turned to see a shapely honey-blonde in a Rolling Stones T-shirt, green running shorts with a slight slit up the sides, and tennis shoes.

"That's me."

"People just call you B?"

"The name's Brett. And yours?"

"Patty."

"Nice to meet you, Patty. You live here too?"

"Third floor. Apartment 312."

"That's an invitation?"

"Sure. Why don't you come over tonight for an apartment warming drink and we can go up to the Jacuzzi and unwind."

"Sounds good. I could use it."

"About nine, then."

"Nine."

Patty smiled and walked down the hall to the elevator. Brett loved tanned legs and she had them. The lady knew how to walk.

Brett spent the rest of the afternoon at the library Xeroxing articles in local papers about the Wilshire district crimes. He brought them home and after a pickup dinner, he studied them all carefully.

A picture began to take shape. About six months ago, two gang members were arrested for breaking and entering and the testimony of a local resident had led to their conviction. They were brothers, one over eighteen, the other was sixteen. The older brother was made an example of and given a heavy sentence while the other brother got off with a couple months in a juvenile facility. The witness was the leader of the local senior citizens crime-watch club and his stand was seen as a valiant effort to try to stem crime in the community.

When the younger brother got out of the juvenile facility, he led the gang against the witness, then against other members of the citizen's crime-watch organization. At first, it was just harassment, purse-snatching, knocking people over on their way home, stealing bags of groceries, breaking windows, and no one was seriously injured.

Then the witness's wife was raped. No charges were filed. There was much speculation as to why not, but it was clear that some threat was used against the witness. One paper said that they were told by a friend of the witness that the gang members promised to return and rape his wife again and again until they ran out of gang members. Even if some were arrested, others would take their place.

So, in the face of this seemingly insurmountable threat, the witness moved, only his friends knew where.

Emboldened by this coup, the gang began to commit more serious crimes. Several people were beaten and old women raped. And always, the last words to the victims were that if they reported the crimes to the police, they would be killed.

The most serious crime, however, the incident which had captured Brett's attention, was what had happened a few days ago. Mrs. Jessie Archer, a seventy-year-old widow, was the victim of a rape about a month back. She felt so humiliated by the experience that the threat of death had failed to silence her. She went to the police and was actively helping them in an all-out effort to locate the gang members responsible. She won the public's praise, like that accorded the witness who was run out of town.

Then, just a few days ago, while waiting for a bus early in the morning, she was set on fire. Someone had squirted gasoline on her, thrown a match on her and run away. It all happened quickly. And if there were any witnesses, they had gotten the message. The police knew who did it, but there wasn't a shred of proof. As usual. They were more than sympathetic, they were outraged that such things could happen in their district. But, without the help of witnesses to supply proof, they were almost powerless.

And even if the guilty parties were caught, the ones who were of adult age would be back on the streets—looking for the people who sent them away—in a fairly short time, and the ones who weren't of legal age would be back on the streets even sooner. Not surprisingly, most people figured it was safer to just stay out of the spotlight and take their chances.

Therefore, Brett considered the only real solution to the situation was to disband the gang, once and for all. The hard way, or the easy way.

Chapter 12

Brett changed into swimming trunks, slipped a robe over his shoulders and made his way down to 312.

Patty opened the door wearing the same T-shirt, but instead of the shorts, she wore the bottoms of a string bikini which made a G-string look like a pair of boxer shorts.

"I wondered if you forgot," she said.

"I have a great memory for legs," he said.

"I guess that's a compliment. Come in, come in. Let me get you a drink."

Brett walked in, sat down on her couch and asked for a beer.

"Welcome to the building," she said raising a drink which had a reddish color to it.

"Thanks. With neighbors as friendly as you, I'm sure I'll enjoy it here."

"You from L.A.?"

"No. The midwest. My company transferred me out here. I'm an engineer with a rubber company."

"Hmm. That's interesting," she said politely.

"Not really. What about you?"

"Oh, I was born here. One of the few you'll find, believe me. But I wouldn't live anywhere else. For all its problems and smog, I'm for L.A. all the way."

"What do you do?"

"Uh, I'm a nurse."

"A humanitarian."

"You could look at it that way."

"So, tell me about this building. What have I gotten myself into here?"

"Well, it's a strange mix, let me tell you. There's a lot of old people here; mostly supported by their rich sons; you know the type. There's a guy on the second floor who's a roadie for the Funky Punks. Sometimes he brings the band home with him after a gig and they play a little music."

"Bet the neighbors like that."

"Yeah, it's kinda outrageous—playing music that late in an apartment building. But, what the hell. I like their music. You like music?"

"Some."

"Like what?"

"Jazz mostly. Keith Jarrett, David Sanborn. I like Steely Dan."

"Oh, I like them, too. I've even got a few of their albums. That gives us something in common."

"Guess so."

"You know, when I moved in here I didn't know I was getting into the middle of a gang war," Brett said steering the conversation in a more relevant direction.

"Hey, me either. I mean this stuff is news to me. Six months ago this place was so quiet—except for the second floor—you'd have thought you were living in Cleveland. No offense. Then wow! Things exploded. It's tough out on the streets now. But they leave younger people alone."

"They leave *you* alone?"

"I'm young."

"But you're also quite attractive."

She blushed a little and said, "Why thank you, Brett." She laughed a nervous laugh. "You want to go up to the Jacuzzi now?"

"Sure."

They went upstairs to the roof where the city had come on like a Christmas tree. A couple of plastic outdoor chairs were occupied near the Jacuzzi but no one else was in the water. Patty turned the knob next to the elevator and the hot water started bubbling.

"Feels good," Brett said, his body adjusting to the water, which was about 108 degrees.

"I love to come up here at night with a drink and just

let all the day's tension drain from my body. Sometimes it feels like I just leave it all here in the water. When I get out I'm emotionally clean. Kind of like a bath for my mind."

From where Brett now sat he could see a beacon just two blocks away at the corner of La Brea and Wilshire that turned alternately green and red.

An older man Brett took to be in his late fifties walked out of the elevator and around the roof saying hello to everyone. Finally he came over to the Jacuzzi, bent down and said hello to Patty.

"This is a new tenant, Brett Alexander," said Patty introducing Brett to the man. "And this is Sid White. He kind of looks out for everybody around here."

"Pleased to meet you, Brett," said the man extending a muscular right arm with a tattoo of a battleship on it.

"Likewise. Navy?" said Brett tilting his head in the direction of the tattoo.

"That's right. Saw action in the Pacific in WW Two. See you around, Brett," said the man and walked back into the elevator and disappeared behind the closing doors.

"I don't know what some people around here would do without Sid," said Patty. "He's like a father to the girls in the building and, well, a companion to the widows."

"What does he do? Around here?"

"He's retired. He and a friend of his from the police force —he's retired too—give self-defense classes every Tuesday night. For free. It gets them a lot of free meals, though. I don't think Sid ever cooks for himself. But that's fair. And it makes a lot of people feel safe to know he's around. Why, whenever there's trouble, everyone calls Sid before they call the manager. A real pantywaist, that guy is. Mr. Sanford. You met him when you paid your deposit."

"Seemed like a nice enough guy to me," said Brett taking a sip of beer from the can.

"Oh, he's a nice guy, but he's helpless. He's as afraid of what's going on as the little old ladies in the neighborhood."

"What do you think's going to happen with this gang violence?"

"I don't know. It's kind of depressing. There doesn't seem to be an end in sight. Some people just get pleasure out of making other people scared, I guess. Maybe they get so little respect at home or out in society, they scare people into giving it to them."

"Maybe. But it's hard to sympathize with people who can be so brutal; especially when you've seen their handiwork up close."

"Sounds like there's a story there," Patty said.

"Nah, not really," said Brett polishing off his beer.

There was a strained moment of silence.

"I'm beginning to feel like a boiled lobster," he said finally.

"Me too. You want to come down for another drink?"

"It's been a tough day. You know, getting oriented to a new place. And I've got to get up early tomorrow morning. Maybe another night. How about tomorrow night? My place?"

Her smile slipped back into gear and she said, "Sure."

"I'll even fix you dinner."

"No, that's not necess—"

"Think nothing of it. I like to cook. And cooking for one just doesn't make it. Tomorrow at, say, seven."

"Got yourself a date."

Brett escorted Patty back to her apartment and went back up to his, changed clothes, went downstairs to the directory and got Sid White's apartment number.

"Sid," said Brett as the retired Navy man opened the door.

"Brett," said White smiling politely. "I pride myself on remembering people's names. I have a theory about that," he said as he stepped back and motioned for Brett to come in. He shut the door and continued. "When you're introduced to somebody, you're usually so worried about how you look to that person that you're not really paying much attention to anything else. So when you hear somebody's name, you're not really listening. Probably a crock, but it makes sense to me. Sit down, sit down."

Brett sat down on the couch.

"I saw you drinking a beer. How about another cold one?"

"Sure. But I don't like to drink alone."

"Don't worry about that."

Sid got two beers from the refrigerator, popped both tops

and handed one to Brett. "To a happy stay here at the Cloverdale." Both men raised their beers toward each other.

Brett could see why Patty felt safer with Sid in the building. Brett didn't know the guy well, but he had good instincts about people. This guy was a no-nonsense, old-school tough who was still sharp, real sharp; the kind of guy who felt a sense of responsibility for his neighbors. Put twenty of these guys on the streets in every neighborhood, thought Brett, and the only crime you'd see would be parking violations.

"So what can I do for ya?"

"Oh, nothing much. Patty said you conduct a self-defense class every Tuesday night. If I'm free I'd like to sit in. Can you tell me anything about it?"

"Nothing much to tell. A buddy a' mine and myself teach a little basic karate to some of the residents. You know anything about the martial arts?"

"I took a class or two here and there. Not much though," said Brett with a straight face. "So any Tuesday night I'm free I can just come on down and join right in?"

"Any Tuesday around seven. If you're out of shape or aren't really smooth on the basics, we'll try to get you caught up fast. But you look like you keep fit. There're so many easier targets in the neighborhood, I'm sure you're not gonna have any trouble."

"Just like to be on the safe side."

"That's the way to be. What's your line, Brett?"

"I'm an engineer for a rubber company out here. I was transferred from Indiana. I like the weather, but I'm not really oriented yet. Don't know many people. Patty was the first person I met."

"Yeah, that Patty," he said with a laugh. "She's a hot number. She's all Charlie's Angels rolled into one heaven-sent sweet thing, all right."

"She's that for sure. Says she's a nurse," Brett said, knowing pretty much how this comment would be greeted by White.

He laughed. "Uh huh. She can heal me any day. Hell, she's no nurse, son. But I have a feeling you know that already."

"Yeah, but it doesn't bother me."

"Hell no. It doesn't bother me either. And I'm not talking bad behind her back. She's one hell of a sweetheart, all right. Let me hear somebody say something bad about her and they'll have my fist for supper. So she's a hooker. I like a person who enjoys their work and does it well, and hell if I can think of anyone who could do it better." He laughed and tossed back another sip of brew.

"You interested in her?"

"Just met her," said Brett. "Seems friendly enough. I'm a pretty good judge of character, and I think she'd be a good friend to have."

"You're right. I've known Patty for a couple years now and if somebody's in a jam, Patty's first in line with the help. And I mean help. Some people'll give you lip service, offer things they know you won't take them up on. Not Patty. If you're a friend of hers and you need what she's got, it's as good as yours."

They both laughed a little at the thought of her having something they both wanted.

"Seems like a pretty diverse mix of tenants here."

"Sure is. We got probably sixty percent who are retirement age or better. A real melting pot. There's Patty, and she's not the only working girl living here. There's a rock group living on the second floor."

"Patty told me about them."

"Yeah, she likes that kind of music. Not me. I'm Country and Western all the way. Then there's quite a few single men like yourself. All in all a hell of an interesting group."

"And Mr. Sanford."

"Oh hell, yes. We call him Mr. Whipple. Truth is, son, he's seen his better days. Used to be in the movie business; or that's how he tells it. I hear he used to be a prop man or somethin' and maybe got a few extra parts in the fifties. He's about fifty-five now. Kinda faggy, if you'll excuse my French. He's an all right guy, but not the kind a' guy the tenants can depend on. If there's trouble, they call me before they call him. Takes all kinds, though, eh slim?"

"Right. Hey, what the hell's going on around this neighborhood?"

"Good question. I'll tell one thing—it's bad. This gang has the locals scared shitless. Can't blame 'em either. Some heavy things have gone down. But I imagine you've heard most of the stories."

"Who's responsible?"

"Near as anyone can figure, it's a gang called the Rangers."

"I've read about the incidents in the newspaper, but I've never seen that name before."

"I got a buddy who's an editor at the local paper; just a weekly, no L.A. Times or anything fancy like that. He's the guy in the know on this thing. Take it from me. He talks to the cops who're handling the case and they tell him a lot that isn't for publication, if you know what I mean."

"Sounds like an interesting guy to know," said Brett sipping his beer.

"And one hell of a nice guy. We served together, him and me. Been friends almost forty years now. And the guy can drink. But then, he's a writer and you know writers. Alcohol, that's the publishing disease, or so he tells it."

"I used to do a little writing in college. Worked on the paper in school for a few years. You know, I'd love to stop by and see how a big city paper really functions."

"I'm tellin' you, it's no big city paper. It's just a local weekly. Probably like a million you got back in Indiana. But I'll tell you what. You look like a guy who doesn't mind a little serious drinking now and again."

"I would qualify as a writer in *that* regard."

"Well then, it's settled. My buddy, Ollie Neal—that's his name—he comes by after the self-defense class every Tuesday—that's day after tomorrow—and we hit a choice little bar a few blocks over on Wilshire. You come along."

"Be glad to."

"Then you and Ollie can talk about the publishing business. He's a talker, that Ollie. You get him going about newspapers and he'll never shut up."

"Sounds good," said Brett draining the last of his brew from the can and standing up. "Thanks for the drink and the company. Nice to meet you, Sid." He extended his hand and the older man met him halfway.

"See you Tuesday night, then," said White getting up and walking his guest to the door.

"Good night," said Brett.

Brett decided he wanted to get a feel for the street at night, smell the turf, get a firsthand look at the playing field. He went back to his apartment and changed into a pair of black pants, a black jacket and stuffed a black cap in his pocket, just in case.

Not surprisingly, the streets were almost deserted. He stopped into the doughnut shop again and the same woman was there.

"Hi," he said. "Long hours."

"Got nights the rest of the week. Glazed and coffee, am I right?"

"The lady's got a memory."

"I was on the all-city doughnut team three years in a row." She smiled.

"Just the city? I'd have thought at least all-state."

"Politics, you know."

She served him his doughnut and coffee and went back to placing fresh doughnuts in their proper display trays.

"Name's Brett."

"Molly. Everybody calls me Molly. Not my real name, but it fits, you know. You gettin' your bearings a little more now? You looked a little lost before."

"Doesn't fit like a glove yet, but it's coming along. Where is everybody? Looks like a ghost town. This isn't how I pictured L.A."

"Well, it's what we were talking about this morning. People are scared."

"But I've been walking around and I haven't seen anybody. Not even hoodlums."

"Yeah, well people are just real cautious. Hell, TV is catching on again. I'll tell you one thing—I make a hell of a lot less doughnuts than I used to at night."

They made small talk for a few minutes, then Brett finished his repast and left.

The streets *were* deserted and the only business open besides the doughnut shop was an all-night gas station. Brett was hoping one of the punks would attack him, but he knew that possibility was extremely unlikely. What had White said? *So many easier targets.*

Brett had just turned back down Cloverdale Avenue when he heard the siren.

Instinctively he turned and ran in the direction of the sound. He hit the corner of Wilshire and Cloverdale and saw two patrol cars, red lights flashing, parked in front of the donut shop. "Shit!" he said aloud and took off running toward the scene.

He stopped running about fifty yards from the action. He knew cops and he didn't want to come *running* onto the scene of a crime. Too many questions and often, understandably, some trigger-happy cops.

The harsh crackle of the police radio split the chilly night air. It was the music of trouble. People didn't use a police radio to deliver birthday greetings. Brett blended into an already forming crowd of about ten to fifteen other people, mostly people who could have heard or seen the police cars from their apartments. People were more willing to come out when the police were there in numbers. And, deep down, below the fear, some of them cared.

Brett cared. About Molly. She wasn't a close friend, but she seemed like a survivor. He liked her. *Damn!*

He moved in a little closer and was just able to see inside the shop. Then he saw her. Her face was covered with a coat, her white dress was torn to shreds and she was lying in a pool of blood.

Brett turned away. He'd conditioned himself those nine years in Japan not to always equate death, even brutal death, with what happened to his family. He would never totally disassociate the two, but at least now it didn't make him violently ill. He had learned to be able to differentiate; no matter how similar, no two incidents were exactly the same. But still . . .

He walked slowly back down Wilshire to Cloverdale then upstairs to his apartment. He fixed himself an Absolut which had been chilling in the freezer, sat down, put on a John Klemmer album and settled back in a slouching position in a chair, feet up on the ottoman.

There would be no witnesses. The street had been deserted. Brett was the only one out walking. Hell, they must have waited for me to leave, thought Brett. Maybe if he—No, that wouldn't get him anywhere.

Brett had put himself in the eye of the hurricane. But then he'd known what was going to happen. He'd planned it that way. But planning it and having it happen were two entirely different things.

Brett went to bed. He didn't sleep right away. When he did he dreamed about women and death and drowning. But the water wasn't water at all; it was his own tears.

Brett awoke about seven and turned on the local all-news radio station. Molly's death was the top story and, as usual, police had no clues. The newsman gave a brief obligatory bio and concluded that Molly was survived by a daughter in Fresno.

Brett whipped up an eye-opener drink consisting of vitamins, some wheat germ, lecithin and fresh fruit.

The thing that bothered Brett most was that he still didn't have a plan. He was hoping to take advantage of opportunities that came his way. But he still didn't have an opening. And things were getting worse. One thing that bothered him about Molly's murder, besides the fact that he liked her, was that she didn't fit the pattern. She wasn't a doddering old woman. There were easier marks. But they went after her. Maybe they were becoming more bold.

Chapter 13

"I can't remember the last time a man cooked supper for *me*," said Patty as Brett set a plate of linguine with white clam sauce in front of her.

"How does it feel?"

"Great," she said smiling widely. "And you made this all from scratch?"

"The clams were made by someone else," he kidded, "but yeah, all from scratch."

"How come a nice guy like you isn't married?"

"Oh, I don't know."

"Ever been married?"

Brett paused and he felt a funny feeling in the pit of his stomach. "No," he recovered. "Guess I'm just a bachelor at heart."

"Probably couldn't find a woman who could cook as well as you do."

"Maybe that's it," he said good-naturedly and sat down. He poured wine and made a toast. "To you. The beauty queen of the Cloverdale apartment complex."

Patty blushed and drank her wine.

"When do you work again?" Brett said, making conversation.

"Ah, well, I kind've have my own hours. It's a great job that way. Doesn't tie me down, you know. I like my freedom."

"Sounds like the best of both worlds. You obviously make good money, and don't have to work nine to five."

Patty started to say something and then looked Brett in the eyes. "I'd say you're a pretty sharp guy."

"Thanks."

"I mean, pretty perceptive."

"Thanks," he said again, knowing what she was building up to.

"I'm not fooling you, am I?" she said seriously.

"No."

"But you still asked me down for dinner."

"Yes."

"Why?"

"Why not?"

"Right. Why not," she said, her smile reappearing full-blown. She took another long sip of wine.

"You're not gay are you?"

"No," said Brett smiling. "I think you're very attractive and I hope that we'll end up having wonderful sex together."

"That's pretty straight."

"Well, you were wondering why I wasn't all over you, weren't you?"

"The thought occurred to me when I asked you down for a drink last night and you didn't come. I don't do that very often."

"I'm sure you don't."

"So how do you like the linguine?" he said changing the subject.

"Great. Really."

During dinner they talked about their childhoods, their prom nights—what disappointments they were—about L.A. and where they'd each like to live someday.

"Can I ask you a question?"

"Sure. I don't have to answer, do I?"

"No," said Brett. "It would seem to me that in the business you're in, you get a lot of street news."

"Street news?"

"You know, what's going on in the street. Often before the cops."

Her smile disappeared. "Why would that interest an engineer for a rubber company?"

"I'm no undercover cop, if that's what you're thinking," said Brett sensing a wall go up.

"In my business, you gotta get a feel for a guy real fast. get good feelings from you, but I'll give you odds you're olding back."

"But you don't feel I'm going to do you any harm, do ou?"

"No."

"Then maybe that's all you have to know."

"Maybe. Maybe not."

"Do you hear things from the street?"

"Look," said Patty seriously. "That communication works oth ways, and it carries with it a lot of responsibility. ometimes I've *got* to know what cooks. So I get the straight uff. When I pass along that privileged communication to he wrong people, it don't look good. People get mad. Some eople get worse than mad."

Brett tried to take the pressure off. "I've just been think- g about what happened last night to Molly at the dough- ut shop."

"Oh God, that was a damn shame. Everybody liked Molly. hat was uncalled for."

"Patty, this whole reign of violence is uncalled for. lothing fair about it."

"I hope you're not planning to play Wyatt Earp."

"Why do you say that?"

"Hey, these dudes aren't kin or nothin', but I know nough about them to know they'd have somebody like you or lunch. And they'd lick the plate. They're animals, Brett. A lot of stuff comes out in the paper. But a lot more doesn't. .eave it alone. The police will eventually nail these assholes."

"But you feel safe?"

"Yeah, as safe as anybody. But, like you say, I know he street. Favors here and there to call in. Plus, most im- ortantly, I'm one careful lady. I might not strike you that vay, but I've been living off my instincts since I was seven- een and I can smell trouble just as sure as if it were a pile f shit sitting in front of me. And you, well, you're not rouble. At least not for me."

"All right," said Brett resignedly. There was an opening here, but it would close up fast if he pushed too hard. He'd vait as long as he could.

"Dessert?"

"I didn't know you made dessert, too," said Patty returning to her lighthearted self.

"I didn't. I thought we'd make that together."

There was nothing on the morning news about more violence in the Wilshire district and Molly's story was absent from news coverage except for a letter to the editor in the Herald Examiner.

The day was uneventful except for the fact that the phone was installed.

Sid White's self-defense class was interesting for Brett to watch. White and his ex-cop buddy were teaching resident moves Brett had learned when he was eight years old. They were as natural to him now as breathing. It was considered common knowledge among the Ninja inner circle when Brett left Japan that he was among the top five Ninja practitioners in the world, which would make him a hundred times more deadly than the top martial artist in the U.S.

White saw Brett come into the class and tried to creep up on him from behind and playfully make a move. But by the time White's hands had begun their outward reach, Brett had instinctively whirled and was holding the older man by the wrist and had to stop a deadly thrust with his other hand. Reflexes.

Brett smiled and tried to slough it off.

"How did you . . ."

"I heard you sneaking up on me."

"But you couldn't have. I . . ."

"It's nothing. I saw you come in and figured you were going to pull something like that."

"But the wrist lock?"

"Instinct. I told you. I took a few classes before."

"Hell you aren't . . ."

A voice interrupted the two. It was White's friend ex-L.A.P.D. officer Jerry Clark. "May I have your attention, please! All right now, let's pair off and go through the drills."

The class did just that and White grabbed Brett by the arm and led him off to the side while Clark led about twenty mostly elderly students in self-defense drills.

"Hey look, son, I'm not going to pry. I didn't live this

96

ong putting my nose into other people's business. But I ust want you to know that you ain't foolin' me."

"About what?" Brett played dumb.

"A hold is one thing, a defensive move can be taught in any karate school. But just a few minutes ago you did something else. You don't learn it going to class once a week or taking classes in the service. I just want to know one thing."

Brett looked at him hard, trying to size him up and said, "What's that?"

"If you're who and what I think you are, you'll tell me straight."

"What's that?" Brett repeated.

"Do I have anything to fear from you?"

"No. Unless you happen to be responsible for the gang violence around here."

"Okay. I feel better already."

"But . . ."

"But what?"

"This goes no further. And I mean *no* further. Not good buddies, newspapermen, ex-cops, lovers, nobody. Understood?"

"Understood. I couldn't prove it anyway."

"But it would get in my way."

"I won't get in your way, son. Hell, you just might be the only damn hope a lot of these people got left. And if I can be of any help . . ."

"We're still meeting your friend who works for the newspaper, right?"

"Him and Jerry," said White tilting his head in the direction of Jerry Clark who was just then showing an old woman how to deliver a knee to an attacker's groin.

"What I don't understand is, what in the hell is somebody like you doing with a small potatoes deal like this?"

"No questions, Sid. It's better that way. And as far as it being small potatoes, I'm looking at about twenty people who consider it the most important thing in the world. A message has got to be delivered, and it might as well go out from here."

Brett watched the class from afar for the most part, then

at White's subtle insistence, he joined White and Clark in showing the group a few simple things to do with an attacker's fingers to cause him pain. The accent was on particular pressure points and vital areas which could be attacked by a weaker individual during an attack.

And while Brett was more than happy to give any assistance he could, he knew most of it would be useless during an actual attack for several reasons. First, all the routines were practiced in an atmosphere where no fear existed. When a person is attacked, especially for the first time, almost nothing but fear exists initially. Secondly, the strength of most attackers was much greater than an elderly person's strength. Further, most attackers carried weapons, and fighting back against a guy who knows how to use a gun or a knife could be fatal.

Still, it was something. They would feel more confident when they walked out of class. They would feel as though they were doing something to protect themselves. That, thought Brett, was the only real benefit.

In Brett's case, however, he had to pass many tests before becoming a full-fledged Ninja. Many times skilled practitioners came at him with weapons raised, more than one attacker at a time, and he had successfully defended himself. He could go into almost any room in the average home and, where apparently no weapons existed, Brett would be able to lay his hands on usually no less than twenty items he could use as lethal weapons. And that didn't include his fingers, hands, arms and legs, with which he could crack open a skull, hook out an eyeball, rip out a heart, castrate an enemy, break bones, and puncture vital organs. And then there were the more esoteric techniques. For example, he could touch a person at a particular place on the forearm—usually without the victim knowing it—and that person would die hours, or even weeks later. This he knew because of his acupuncture healing training, which was then simply applied in reverse. There were other things he could do. And Brett almost always had the element of surprise. For even if someone surprised him, that person didn't know what a world of hurt they were getting themselves into.

Brett had been a good martial artist when he left the States nearly a decade before. But he was a master's master now.

He was at a place where other masters could only imagine. But he was not alone. There were a few others, no more than five, who were where Brett was technically and mentally. And that was something Brett never forgot.

"So Brett, Sid tells me you're a new tenant over on Cloverdale," said Jerry Clark.

"That's right. Company transferred me here from Indiana. Looks like I might have come at the wrong time, though."

"How's that?" asked Ollie Neal.

"This gang violence thing. It's depressing. I just met the woman who was killed the other night. In fact, I was in there not a half hour before it happened."

"Hell of a thing, hell of a thing," said Clark.

Four drinks were delivered to the table. Three beers and an Absolut for Brett.

"Let me get the first round," said Brett reaching for his wallet.

"No way, son," said White grabbing his arm. This is your initiation. First-timers don't pay all night. You'll get your chance to pick up a few next week."

"Them's the rules," said Neal. "Welcome to L.A.," he said raising his glass of beer in a toast to Brett.

They all touched glasses and toasted Brett.

"Mind if I ask you a few questions, Mr. Neal?" said Brett.

"Ollie."

"Ollie. I don't know much about the newspaper business, but I do know a little. Don't you hear a lot more than you can actually print?"

"What are you getting at?"

"I mean, a lot of times the cops or an informant will give you some info you're sure is on the up and up, but, since there's no real way to prove it, you sit on it until you can back it up."

"That's true. What do you want to know? Who really killed Kennedy?" said Neal with a smile.

"I already know that," said Brett smiling in return. "No, seriously, I'm curious about this gang business. For instance, I know that you can't name a juvenile in a newspaper account, but that doesn't stop cops and some newspaper people from knowing the names. This whole gang business, it just keeps getting worse."

"You're right. But you read the papers and watch TV. You *know* the *real* problem. This community lives in fear. No one wants to testify against any of these punks. And who can blame them. Even if they're convicted, they're not going in for very long and when they get back out they'll come looking for the person who sent them away."

"Can't the police at least put on a visual display, be more visible?"

"There are problems with that," interjected ex-cop Jerry Clark. "First of all, there's a shortage of manpower to handle the street these days. And if you flood the streets—like they did in the Valley not long ago, and as they did here a few weeks ago—things get real quiet. Problem is, you just can't *keep* every street flooded with armed men. This isn't the only war zone in the city, and there just isn't enough manpower to go around."

"I'll tell you what," said White half under his breath so he couldn't be heard by others sitting at nearby tables. "I'd like to catch one of those sons-of-bitches alone one night. I'd take the fight out of his act."

"That's one of the problems, though, Sid," said Neal taking another sip of his beer. "You're *not* going to catch one of these guys alone. They're brutal assholes, but they're not stupid."

"I still think some kind of neighborhood watch program would help. Maybe it wouldn't handle the whole problem, but I think it would help."

"Back to my original question, Ollie," said Brett. "Do the police actually know who these guys are?"

"From what I hear—sometimes that's a lot, sometimes it isn't—they call themselves the Wilshire Rangers and they hang out in the Crenshaw district, which borders the Wilshire district to the south. Two ex-cons pull the strings, but they're smart as hell. Its memberships run about fifty percent black, thirty percent brown, and the rest white.

"In fact, it's a pretty slick operation. The two leaders, Poppa Williams, a black guy with arms the size of trees, and Angelo Bandini, a tough from the East who met Williams when they were both in San Quentin, have a team of lawyers and accountants that would rival the IRS. Both guys are in their mid-thirties. *Officially*—and I use the word very loosely here—the Wilshire Rangers are a religious youth group that does work to raise money for poor kids' lunch programs and summer camps, you know. Fact is, there've been more than a few politicians taken in by the scam."

"What does all this have to do with violence against these old people?" asked Brett genuinely puzzled.

"Well, it's not all as random as the press would have you believe. This whole thing started about six months ago, as I'm sure you read, with the trial of two gang members. Those gang members were actually Williams's younger brothers. One was under age and the other is still in jail—and will be for a couple more years; at least that's what the judge had in mind. Nowadays you never know. Anyhow, Williams had sent one of his lieutenants to pay a visit to the witness, Ira Moskowitz, to tell him that it would be better for everybody concerned if Ira would tell the jury that there was a 'shadow of a doubt' in his mind about who he really saw breaking into his house. But Moskowitz was the head of the senior citizens' crime-watch club and he decided to make a stand. The night before the trial Williams himself showed up at a crime-watch meeting, at which Moskowitz was presiding, and tried to make the message more clear. Moskowitz refused to be buffaloed and the club verbally backed him up and called Williams a 'nigger punk' and told him to get out of their neighborhood.

"That wasn't the smartest thing they ever did. After Williams's brothers were convicted, Mrs. Moskowitz was raped and the threat came down that it wouldn't be the last time. Moskowitz moved—can't blame him, really—and then a lot of 'random' violence started occurring in the district. And now no one in their right mind is going to testify against Williams or any one in the gang."

"Tell me more," said Brett sipping on his Absolut.

"Well, on the surface they do all these good things for kids. They raise their money by sponsoring car washes, things like that, but their real money comes from drugs and prostitution. Fact is, all this publicity is doing them a lot of good. Sure, their name isn't mentioned on the air, but their street competitors know. They don't need a program to tell what's going on.

"And they're shrewd as hell. For instance, if they want someone hit, or need a job done that carries a heavy ticket if their man gets caught, they get fifteen, sixteen, seventeen-year-olds to do the job. That way, the job gets done and nobody pays a heavy toll. They're slick.".

"What about the cops? They can't be just rolling over and playing dead on this," said Brett.

"Look," said Clark, "recent laws regarding use of the choke hold, plus the media's whining about 'police brutality' have taken a lot of weapons out of the cops' hands. Hell, not only do these guys outnumber us, they also have more legal weapons to use against us than we have to use against them. It's a damn shame. I never thought it would come to this. Shit!" said Clark disgustedly as he downed a few more gulps of beer.

"How powerful are Bandini and Williams?" asked Brett.

"They're connected, if that's what you mean."

"I mean what would happen to the group without Bandini and Williams?"

"Let me put it this way, a lot of politicians and a few cops would breathe a lot easier if they weren't around."

"What would happen to the gang?"

"It would disappear."

"How can you be sure?"

"The gang, the army, so to speak, has been there for years. It'll be there after those two. But the difference is Williams and Bandini. These guys wrote the book on streetwise. They know how to organize, how to lead, how to pimp, how to deal. They whipped a band of uncontrollable ruffians into a smooth-running army. A lot of their strength comes from image. They do *what* they want, *when* they want, and nobody raises a finger against them. The peons see this and they're impressed. They'll follow the king of the hill. Right now Williams and Bandini are kings of the hill and that fact cannot be disputed. And that's why there's no stopping them."

"But your theory is, if someone *did* stop Williams and Bandini, that would do the trick."

"Yeah. But that's one big if. They're too sharp to let

anything happen to them. They delegate illegal actions and insulate themselves just like the Mafia. And as far as walking in and trying to knock one of them off, it'd be easier to assassinate the President of the United States."

"Why was someone like Molly killed?"

"Molly was part of the senior citizen's crime-watch group."

"And, God rest her soul," said White, "she had a big mouth."

"What do you mean?"

"Well, for one thing, she spoke to anyone and everyone about how she thought the gang was a bunch of punks who ought to be taken out and shot. She was too visible. And you never know if you're talking to the wrong person."

"That's true," said Neal. "Not all the members of the group are black and walk around with headbands and T-shirts announcing they're part of the Wilshire Rangers."

"How do they recruit members?" asked Brett.

"You don't go sign up, I can tell you that," said Neal, draining the last of his beer from the glass.

"They come to you," explained Clark. "You come to their attention in a bad or good way, and they come to you with an offer to join."

"I take it that it's an offer without too many options."

"That's right. The options are few and clearly spelled out."

"Usually," continued Neal, "a new member is recommended by a member or somebody who knows a member."

"So when do you think things are going to cool down here?"

"It's anybody's guess," said Clark. "Nobody knows. Right now the current violence is probably spearheaded by Williams's younger brother, Terrence, as a personal vendetta and Poppa Williams has no reason to stop it. It isn't hurting anything and it helps in the form of intimidation. There's even the strong possibility that if the old people move out of here—and there's some indication that that's happening already—then, since it's a pretty nice area in which to live, younger people will begin moving into the area and a lucrative drug market will be created. Already the population of under-thirties has risen from ten percent six months ago to about fifteen percent. It was happening slowly anyway, but this seems to be accelerating the process."

"This is all old news, though," said White taking a deep sigh and exhaling. "The bottom line is, we're still back at the same damn place. We just don't know what the hell to do about it."

"That's the truth," said Clark sadly.

"Yeah," said Neal.

"Maybe not," said Brett softly. Neal and Clark didn't even hear him say it. But White did and he turned and looked into Brett's eyes. White didn't say anything, but the hairs on the back of his neck stood on end. And for the first time since the trouble started, Sid White *didn't* feel that things were hopeless after all.

Chapter 14

Brett and Sid White walked home. Brett had asked him not to question him earlier and White wanted to help Brett in any way he could. And in order to do that he would need to get Brett to trust him. He would let Brett ask the questions.

"Nice guys," said Brett as they walked down the deserted streets of Wilshire Boulevard.

"Salt of the earth, and that's for sure. And I know they liked you, too. I can tell."

"Sid."

"Yes, Brett?"

"Let me ask you a hypothetical question."

"Shoot," said White, taking a pack of cigarettes out of his pocket and lighting up as they walked past a dark Woolworth's store.

"What if you knew somebody who wanted to become a member of the Wilshire Rangers? What would you tell him to do?"

"That, I can't help you—I mean your friend—with. Hell, I got no idea whatsoever."

"Then what about the area where they operate? Think it would do any good to hang around there?"

"Don't know that either. If you ask me, it sounds like an easy way to get hurt. For most people," he said smiling slyly at Brett.

"How do I get there from here?"

White stopped and turned so that he was facing La Brea. "Go down to La Brea and turn right, that's south, and just follow that down to Folsom Street. It's a major cross street, you can't miss it. There's a big burger joint on one corner and a topless and bottomless place on the other. That's Ranger turf."

"Thanks, Sid."

"You want to stop by my place for a nightcap?" asked White as the two arrived at the Cloverdale Apartments.

"No thanks. I'm not tired. I think I'll go out for awhile."

"And maybe catch a topless show while you're at it?"

Just as Brett and White were coming in, Patty was going out. She looked sexy in a red wrap-around dress, and white high heels. She looked at them with a face that'd make any guy wish he had some money to spend.

"You guys done already? The night's just begun."

"Not for me," said White a little too wearily, the way people getting old often exaggerate when talking to someone much younger.

"And how about you?" she said to Brett.

"Got a busy day tomorrow. Have fun," he said politely ending the conversation. Brett had business on his mind.

"See you all later," said the honey-haired hooker and disappeared through the front door. She walked down the steps and White mumbled some admiring words as the elevator doors closed upon the front lobby.

Brett didn't know exactly what his plan was or how to dress for the occasion. He put on a pair of good jeans—couldn't go wrong there—a T-shirt, a tweed sports coat, and a white pair of jazz dance shoes. The shoes were a unique eccentricity of dress he'd picked up recently when a dancer friend of his had told him that he'd had a pair of the soft shoes fitted with street soles. Brett had tried it and now always kept a pair around. And they looked good, too.

Brett followed White's instructions and turned right on Folsom off of La Brea and cruised the area It was a sea of activity. Prostitutes were openly leaning in cars, their skirts riding up from behind as they did, revealing the unwrapped goods, making their deals. Cadillacs driven by wide-brimmed pimps glided in and out of the various all-night establishments on the boulevard. There was a mixture of blacks, whites, and Latins, so Brett didn't look *that* suspicious when he parked his car and went into the Brass Ball for a drink and a look at the "Live Nude Girls."

He ordered a beer, sat a few rows from the stage and watched Alexandra the Great go through her paces with some Ping-Pong balls on stage.

All the while, over the din he tried to hear some of the conversations around him, listening for talk about the Wilshire Rangers.

He nursed the Coors beer and listened for about a half hour without any luck. Then, after the music stopped and the girl collected her Ping-Pong balls, conversations could be heard more clearly. Brett heard someone mention the name Bandini.

"So Bandini's s'posed to get back to me next week," one white guy was saying to a black guy.

"No shit, man! Well that *is* heavy. I mean that is *very* heavy."

"We'll see, we'll see. Bandini jacked me around before. We'll see," said the man and chugged the remaining half of his beer.

Several scenarios went through Brett's mind as he contemplated various courses of action. It would be easy to start a fight, beat a tough guy to a pulp, and be noticed. But Brett had the feeling he was dealing with people who hadn't just ridden into town on the back of a covered wagon. Bandini and Williams were sharp and they wouldn't be fooled by something that obvious.

Such blatant heroics were better left to Clint Eastwood; they were not suited to a Ninja.

Another possible scenario would be for Brett to pose as a drug dealer or buyer, or as someone looking for a prostitute. But, for tonight at least, he didn't feel he looked the part.

No, tonight was just to get a feel for things. He ordered another beer, sat back, waited for the next act, and kept an ear open.

"Bandini's coming here? Tonight? Not shit!" said a black man sitting near Brett.

"That's the straight stuff, brother," said a white man.

"The man, hisself. Go on, you jive-ass. What's he comin' here for, dude?"

"Me and him's got business."

"You and the *man?* Don't make me laugh, honky."

"Look man, don't believe me. Don't make me no difference. He's comin' here soon, too. You'll believe me when he walks through the door."

"When he walks through the door? Yeah, I'll believe that."

"You care to put any money on it?"

"Hell. You lyin' man, and I'm gonna make me ten on that," said the black man and took out his wallet and laid a ten-dollar bill on the table. The white man did the same thing and laughed.

The next dancer came on and was introduced as Bo Drake, the MC slurring the "D" and the "R" a little. Bo came on stage looking a little like the perfect ten herself in braided and beaded hair. But the resemblance stopped there and became even more remote when the clothes started coming off. The real item was still under twenty-one and this girl didn't look like she'd seen the friendly side of twenty-five for some time.

She came and went without much fanfare and when the music stopped the black guy and the white guy were still at it.

Finally the white guy said, "All right! Pay up fool." He directed the other guy's attention to a man who'd just walked in the front door.

"That's Bandini, all right," said the black guy. "I'll be damned."

"You can count on that," said the other cheerfully and picked up the two ten-dollar bills lying in the center of the table.

Angelo Bandini was a muscular, dark-skinned Italian with the stereotypical Roman nose. He wore a blue tailored sports coat, beige slacks, beige Hush Puppy shoes, a small-collared shirt Brett recognized to be a Pierre Cardin, and a ring on his right hand that would choke a Pittsburgh Steeler linebacker. He was accompanied by two blacks, one on either side, who wouldn't be able to walk through garage doors side by side.

Bandini stopped a few feet inside the Brass Ball and one of the bodyguards went upstairs. After a minute or two, the bodyguard came down and whispered something in Bandini's ear and the trio went upstairs.

As the Italian and the two thugs passed by Brett's table, the white man who'd been talking about his meeting with Bandini tried to say something to the Italian, but Bandini just walked on by.

After the Italian had been upstairs for a few minutes, the man with the alleged meeting went upstairs and disappeared into the same room Bandini had gone into.

Brett noticed that there was a telephone next to the door behind which Bandini was holding court. Suddenly Brett remembered somebody he wanted to call, and went upstairs to the phone and dialed his apartment. No one answered, but Brett began a dialogue with the ringing sound in his ear. He was waiting for the door to open.

After about five minutes it did. Just for an instant. Bandini was sitting on a couch across from the white guy who had been sitting next to Brett downstairs. The man was doing a lot of arm waving and Bandini looked very cool and calm. One thing Brett noticed before the door was abruptly closed —a quick flash of a bright red wrap-around dress draped around a pair of nice legs. Brett had seen that dress and those legs before. Just as he and Sid White were coming into the Cloverdale.

Chapter 15

Brett left the Brass Ball shortly after that. He wasn't sure whether or not he was closer to a plan, but he had a sense of the turf now.

Bandini, thought Brett, looked as shrewd as he'd been described to be.

One thing Brett hadn't counted on, was Patty's presence in this thing. Especially in Bandini's camp. Brett would have to approach the subject carefully with Patty if he wanted to get a straight answer. Patty had no idea Brett was dealing himself into the game. And Brett thought it best to keep it that way for the time being.

The next morning Brett was awakened by a loud, insistent knocking at his door. Chances were, it was someone from the building, otherwise his outside buzzer would have sounded first.

He slipped on his olive-and-white-striped Dior robe, padded out of the bedroom, across the thick gold shag carpet, looked through the small peephole in the door, and saw Sid White looking anxious and upset.

Brett turned a couple of the locks and opened the door.

"Sid, what's wrong?"

"Thank God! Thank God! You're all right!"

"Come in, Sid. Tell me what's going on."

Brett ushered his distraught neighbor into his apartment and fixed them each a cup of coffee. "Here, looks like you could use this."

"Brett, you don't know how glad I am to see you looking well."

"What's this all about?"

"Obviously you haven't heard."

"Heard what?"

"The news is full of it this morning. Last night some white guy, who the cops referred to as a 'karate expert,' got the shit kicked out of him by the Rangers. The only reason the guy wasn't killed was because those jackasses got some kind of a sense of humor. Terrence Williams, that's Poppa Williams's little brother, filed assault charges against the guy."

"Who is this 'karate expert'?"

"The reports on the radio were sketchy. I called Ollie as soon as I heard because I thought it was you. He gave me what he knew. The name didn't help 'cause I figured you weren't using your own name anyhow. Ollie told me that from what the cops can gather the guy's the grandson of the woman who was set on fire. Naturally he was appalled by what happened to his grandmother and felt frustrated— like a lot of us—that nothing was being done about it. He's supposed to be some kind of a hotshot martial artist. He figured he'd take these guys on like he was Bruce Lee."

"And he figured wrong."

"Apparently. And to add insult to injury, this smartass Terrence Williams called the cops and, with a pile of witnesses to back him up, made the officers arrest this guy. So now the guy's recuperating in the hospital and when he recovers, he's got to face charges."

"What are the chances of him doing time?" said Brett sipping his coffee.

"Don't know. I asked Ollie about that and he said Williams has got a ballpark full of lawyers who know how to swing the bat. On the other hand the D.A. isn't going to be in any hurry to send this kid away. From what I understand, he's got no priors so he'd probably get off with a suspended sentence, especially since Williams wasn't even hurt."

"Poor kid. I know how he feels."

"Hell, we all do. We would've voted the kid a medal if he'd been successful. Problem is, he wasn't and, if anything, it hurts us psychologically. Because people see that even a guy who's skilled in the martial arts can't go up against the Rangers. Damn, it's a royal mess, and that's for sure," concluded White taking a couple of sips from the pewter mug Brett had given him.

"Any luck last night?"

"What do you mean?" asked Brett innocently.

"Your car was gone about a half hour after we parted company. You turned down an invitation from Patty and you asked me how to get to the Rangers' turf."

"Look Sid," said Brett.

"Okay, okay. I won't pry."

But there was a somewhat strained silence as the two men sipped their morning drinks.

"I saw Bandini," said Brett finally.

White smiled. He felt Brett had made a decision to trust him. Maybe not with everything, but with something and that made Sid feel important. "Tough monkey, that Bandini. Used to be a Golden Gloves boxer. I saw him fight down at the Olympic a few times. Could've gone places, too, except that he killed a guy—not in the ring. Spent a few years in S.Q. for that little number. That's where he met Williams."

"He had two guys with him who looked liked they eat bullets for snacks."

"It's a tough crowd, Brett. In fact, I heard—and I don't know how much of it's really true—but I heard that after Bandini and Williams got together, the two of them organized the yard at S.Q. And the only way the guards could restore order was to parole those two out of there. It's a hell of a thing when they start lettin' people out of jail *because* they're too dangerous there. Hell of a thing."

"I agree," said Brett finishing his coffee and looking decidedly more alert.

"And Williams's younger brother, Terrence, was let out two months early last Spring from a juvenile facility because they didn't have enough room. What in the hell is going on with the corrections system in this country?" said White taking another long pull off his coffee.

"Maybe there's just too much to correct."

"Maybe. Hell, when I was growing up, you were afraid to do illegal things, because sure as shit if you got caught either you were going to jail or the cops would beat hell out of you. Man *those* were the old days.

"And they start so damn young. I've seen some of the Rangers over here walking around like they owned the place and *some* can't be more than twelve years old. I came from a tough neighborhood in Chicago. I didn't live no sheltered childhood and, by God, it *was* different then. It was rough, but *nothin'* like this shit. But what the hell," said White finishing his coffee, setting the mug on the coffee table and pushing it away from him.

"All this doesn't amount to a hill of beans, though, does it, son? I mean what the hell difference does it make? It seems like things are just too far gone to do anything except try to stay out of the line of fire."

"Sometimes I feel that's the truth. But there are other times when I have good reasons to feel more optimistic."

"And this morning?"

"This morning I feel like we're in the middle of a war and we're fighting off oncoming tanks with slingshots. God, I hope we're wrong."

"Me too."

"Sid, how badly is this kid hurt?"

"From what I understand, just a few broken bones, ribs mostly. He should be up and around in a day or two. His face took a little beating, but it's not serious."

"What are the chances of getting in to see him?"

"There's a police guard on the door from what I hear."

"Between Jerry and Ollie, you think you could pull a few strings?"

"Probably not. But I could find out what room he's in if that'll help."

"That would help. Not as much as a free pass, but I'm inventive."

"I'll bet you are," said White grinning for the first time since he came in.

Chapter 16

A policeman sat in a chair on one side of the entrance to room 324. A thermos and a cup rested on the floor on one side of the chair and a pile of newspapers and magazines lay on the other. The cop was reading the sports section of the Herald Examiner when an orderly, nodded and walked into room 324. The cop didn't look concerned. After all, he'd already talked to his "prisoner" and, if anything, he sympathized with the kid. And he wasn't going to escape. Hell, the bond wouldn't be any more than pocket money anyhow. The cop knew the rough look of the Rangers and he'd be especially on the lookout for _that_ type.

"Hi," said Brett to the blond-haired man sitting up in bed watching the news. Brett figured him to be about twenty-two or three; he couldn't tell for sure because the guy's face was badly bruised. He had wide shoulders, and was muscled and toned.

"Hi," the man said. Brett had learned the man's name was Jeff Archer.

"You're kind of a hero around here," said Brett to the patient.

"Some hero. I got beat up and now I might even go to jail."

"Still, somebody ought to do what you did, or at least tried to do. That's what most people are feeling. They're frustrated about crime, but they don't know what to do about it. At least you tried."

"Yeah," said Archer almost as if he didn't care anymore.

Brett knew the feeling. Jeff was depressed. He'd lost faith in himself and in the system. He was disoriented and Brett couldn't blame him. But Brett wanted some information and had to get it fast before someone came in and recognized that he wasn't supposed to be there.

"Mind if I ask you a question?"

"Nah, go ahead," said Jeff in a disinterested manner.

"How the hell did you track that guy down?"

"That was the easy part. I just looked the part for a couple days and hung around the Rangers' turf. Eventually I kept hearing about Williams and his 'spectacular' fete involving my grandmother"—here Archer's voice cracked a little, but he recovered quickly—"and I eventually just traced the talk to the person. He's a pretty visible character. His brother's the brains, along with an Italian guy, but this young punk Terrence is the mouth. Hell, he was easy to find."

"And where was that?"

"Why?" asked Archer, for the first time showing suspicion and really looking at the orderly.

"Just curious."

"Don't get any wild ideas, like trying to be a hero. You're looking at one right now, and believe me I was lucky. If Terrence hadn't been in such a funny mood—they thought it would be a great joke to have me arrested for assaulting *them*—I'd be dead."

"I'm just curious, that's all. I hear he hangs out at the Brass Ball," said Brett trying to steer Archer toward an answer.

"You heard wrong. He hangs out at a place called the Cheshire Cat. It's about a mile from the Brass Ball."

"What actually went down, if you don't mind my asking?"

"No. It's a short story. I tracked Williams to the Cheshire Cat last night, went in and had a few drinks; waiting for him, you know. Anyhow, I finally see him, apparently alone, walking into the place. I walk over and tap him on the shoulder and tell him who I am. He laughs and I start to go at him. Before I land a kick or a punch three other guys are all over me and Williams is just laughing his ass off. Then they try to figure out what to do with me and Williams comes up with his joke. That's about it. I wasn't exactly *walking tall*."

"No, but you tried. And a lot of people admire that."

"Thanks, but the bottom line is that I made a fool of myself and Williams had the last laugh."

"Maybe all the laughing isn't done," said Brett taking Archer's tray full of barely-touched food and turning to go.

Archer looked at Brett and said, "Don't try it, man. You don't know what you're letting yourself in for."

"Have a good day, Mr. Archer," said Brett and left the room. The guard was now working on a mug of steaming coffee. He nodded and grunted something as Brett passed him and walked away down the corridor.

Brett went back to the Cloverdale, took his phone off the hook, and meditated for a couple hours. Then he prepared a simple dinner of rice and vegetables and had two cups of tea while listening to some jazz and relaxing before going out for the evening.

The Cheshire Cat was a little smaller than the Brass Ball and there were no nude dancers. The crowd was again a mixture of blacks, browns, and whites. All the waitresses were black and wore uniforms which consisted of black Danskins over black panty hose, and high heels.

The crowd looked pretty rough, lots of muscles and loud talk. Brett sat at the bar and made small talk with the bartender. Tonight, Brett, unshaven, was dressed in some faded jeans, scuffed tennis shoes, a T-shirt and a brown zipper-up-the-front nylon jacket.

The talk around the place was about Terrence's performance the night before and how he'd made Jeff Archer look "like such a jerk." Terrence was their hero. Brett just breathed evenly, deeply and remained calm. Waiting. Waiting for an opening.

About ten o'clock Terrence Williams came into the Cheshire Cat with a white girl on one arm and a black girl on the other. He was grinning from ear to ear.

"The *man* has arrived!" he announced raising his arms and wagging his head from side to side.

A loud cheer went up from the packed house and he was applauded.

Then Williams made his way to the bar and stood next to Brett. Brett just looked straight ahead into the mirror behind a row of bottles. Their eyes met briefly. For an instant it seemed that Williams's smile flickered then it resumed its original strength. "Drinks all 'round," he announced, and again a hero's cheer went up from the customers.

Williams and the two girls found a booth in the back of the bar and they were joined by a couple of rough types. Drinks were brought to the table and Williams began to talk animatedly to the pair who had just joined them.

Gradually the bar returned to what passed for normal for about a half hour. Then Williams took center stage again.

He stood, moved out into the center of the room and said, "May I have your attention, please! I'd like to thank all those gathered here tonight for this reception and, my friends, there can be no doubt who rules this turf. The Rangers! The Rangers! The Rangers!" Williams began to lead the crowd in a chant that culminated in loud yells and more cheers.

"We're the baddest of the bad, the meanest of the mean. Nobody messes with the Rangers, cause we eat them alive!"

Again the crowd cheered.

"Or else we have them arrested by the pigs!" He laughed aloud and the entire bar joined him.

"I got a special surprise for y'all tonight. Come up here, Candy," said Williams to the white girl who was still sitting at the table he'd just left.

She was reluctant at first, but she eventually made it to Williams's side and he put his arm around her.

"Whatcha think o' this sweet thing, y'all?"

There were loud whistles and howling approval.

"And you ain't seen nothin' yet. Show 'em honey."

The girl just stood there, shaking. Brett could see her arms trembling even from where he sat, twenty feet or more away.

"Some music!" Williams yelled and the jukebox was turned on.

The girl was still shaking when Williams cleared a table in front of him and lifted her onto it. "Do it for Poppa, now," he said sweetly. She resisted. "Do it now!" he said, the sweetness gone from his voice. There was only the command—the threat.

The music started and the girl began to dance. Everyone knew that wasn't all she was expected to do. Her dress came off first, to the wild screams of the customers. Then her bra. But she hedged on her panties. Brett saw her face, tears in her eyes, pleading with Williams to let her stop now. But Williams just stood there grinning.

A few minutes went by, but she still hadn't taken off her panties and Williams's mood was beginning to change. He wanted her nude and wouldn't be happy until she was. He signaled for the music to stop and a hush fell over the bar. All eyes were on Williams and the girl.

"I want you nude. Don't embarrass me in front of my friends, girl. You strip. Nude!" he yelled. "Or else I just might set you on fire like that old lady. You hear me, girl?"

The girl, now in tears, reached down to the waistband of her bikini briefs and lowered them over her hips, down her thighs and stepped out of them. Williams tapped the inside of her leg, indicating to her that she should stand with her legs further apart. She did.

"All right!" said Williams breaking the silence.

The crowd resumed its howling and yelled various vulgar expressions of approval.

"Okay, honey, you did good," Brett heard Williams say as he dismissed the girl and she picked up her clothes and disappeared into the women's restroom.

The whole episode made Brett feel cheap for even having watched it. There were those who thought hell actually existed on earth. At moments like these Brett felt as if there might be some truth to that.

Meanwhile Williams was laughing at the table and being patted on the back by a throng of adoring followers. After about fifteen minutes Williams got up and went to the restroom.

It was now or never. There was no one in the john besides Williams when Brett walked in. Williams had his back to Brett and was using one of the urinals.

"You're a pretty tough guy, Terrence," said Brett to Williams.

Williams grunted something and didn't turn around.

Brett locked the door to the restroom.

"But not that tough."

Williams zipped up his pants and turned around to see what wise guy was preparing to throw his life away.

"What's that?" said Williams turning slowly and chewing on a toothpick dangling out of one side of his mouth.

"I said it doesn't take a tough guy to set an old lady on fire."

"Look chump, I don't know who the fuck you think you are, but let me tell you something. Some honky came in here last night and tried to play hero. I let him live. I ain't feelin' so generous tonight."

"You just push around women, or do you fight *men,* too?"

"You're dead, chump," said Williams moving toward Brett.

Williams pulled a knife and lunged at Brett. Brett grabbed the knife hand, applied enough pressure to make Williams drop the weapon, then broke the man's wrist over his knee. Williams let out a howl, but it was barely audible above the bar noise. Brett knew he didn't have much time, any minute someone would want to use the john and find the door locked. He just took time to say, "Terrence, you're slime. And I'm going to kill you. But I want you to remember as your last thought on Earth that you'd still be alive if you hadn't killed an old lady who—"

"Fuck you, you—"

Brett hit Williams's nose with the palm of his hand and pushed bone and cartilage up into Williams's brain. The big man collapsed, dead in front of the urinal.

Just then Brett heard the door. Someone was trying to get in. There was a small window above the urinal. Brett pulled himself up to it, opened it and pushed himself out into the alley. He pitched forward on his hands, sprang immediately to his feet, ran down the alley to his car in the parking lot, and drove away.

Brett had just delivered a message.

Brett drove home at a normal speed. No need to make himself conspicuous. He was home by ten-thirty. Considering this was the first time he'd done something like this since he executed his parents' killers nearly ten years ago, his nerves weren't too bad.

Brett didn't have to rationalize his behavior to himself.

He knew that there were logical arguments for and against. The men Brett had killed were admitted killers of innocent people. They intended to kill again. The law could apparently do nothing to spare the potential victims. To Brett, society was at war and he was simply doing the responsible thing: stopping murderers from murdering again.

Brett grabbed a crossword puzzle book he'd been working in and retired for the evening, feeling strangely serene, content.

Chapter 17

Brett awoke the next morning around seven, got up, put on his robe, brewed some freshly ground coffee, retrieved the newspaper, and sat down to see if he'd made the news.

In the Metro section on page two there was a brief account of the Williams killing. It had occurred so late that few details had been available, but initially police were labeling it a gang-related killing, which meant that they weren't planning to waste much time finding out who did what they wished somebody would do to the whole bunch.

About eight o'clock Brett called Ollie and asked if he'd like to meet him for lunch. Ollie said sure and they set a time and place.

Brett arrived at the Salt Shaker at noon and looked for Ollie. The newspaperman was already seated at a booth and waved Brett over.

"Nice place," said Brett.

"Oh, it's okay for a quick lunch if you like hamburgers or salad."

"I like both."

The two made small talk for a while, then ordered.

"Hear about Terrence Williams?" said Ollie.

"I saw something in the paper this morning. Not much in the way of facts, though."

"Nobody's got much in the way of facts about this case."

"Why's that?"

"Beats me," said Ollie. "Maybe it was gang-related like

the papers say and nobody's talking. One interesting thing, though."

"What's that?"

"The guy was killed by somebody who knew something about hand-to-hand combat. Like a green beret. Or a karate expert. First person that came to mind was Jeff Archer, that kid whose grandmother was set on fire, the guy who tried to beat Williams up the night before."

"Sounds logical," said Brett sipping his water.

"No dice. Archer was under police guard in the hospital. How about that. Things are heating up."

"So what's going to happen now?"

"What do you mean?"

"Well, you think any heat'll come off the Wilshire district?"

"Hard to tell. It could go either way. It might scare them off, but more likely it'll accelerate the attacks. You see, this whole scare tactic ploy over the past few months has been good PR for the Rangers. Now, if they back off because one of their soldiers bites the dust, all that gain will go to waste. Another thing. Since Terrence was Poppa's little brother, he might get *real* upset. And that would be rough."

"What's your gut feeling?"

"I think it's gonna get rough. Matter of fact, I was going to call Jerry and Sid to talk the situation over. Maybe organize a street patrol, just in case. Hell, I don't know. But it wouldn't hurt to be prepared. You want to come?"

"Sure."

"Great. My place for dinner. Come with Sid. He knows the way."

The food was delivered by a would-be actor, typical of Beverly Hills-Hollywood restaurants and the two ate their meals and discussed the Dodgers.

"Let's take my car," said Brett when he and Sid stepped into the elevator and pressed the button for the garage.

"Fine."

"You know what this meeting is about?"

"Ollie just called me and said he thought it would be a good idea if we all got together. I think it has something to do with the Terrence Williams murder," said Sid looking at Brett out of the corner of his eye.

"Never ask," said Brett, short circuiting what could have been an incriminating discussion.

"Right," said the older man.

The elevator doors opened and the two walked into the garage, to Brett's car, and drove over to Ollie Neal's.

"Beer?" called Ollie from his kitchen.

"Fine with me," shouted Sid.

"Fine with me," chimed Brett.

Jerry Clark had arrived earlier and was already working on his second beer.

Neal came back into the living room and handed out the beers.

"So why the powwow?" said Sid taking a long pull off his brew.

"I thought we ought to talk about what happened last night with Terrence Williams and what it could mean to us living in the Wilshire district."

"What *should* it mean?" asked Clark.

"Well, let me just tell you what I've been able to piece together this afternoon from my sources. As you know, Terrence Williams was killed last night in the restroom of the Cheshire Cat. Police don't give a damn about who did it and aren't busting their asses to find out. The way I hear it, even if they did it wouldn't make any difference. Whoever did it, left no clues. Except that in leaving no apparent clues and in leaving no *doubt* that Williams was killed by a pro, he left the clue that he was dangerous, and that he was around.

"Poppa Williams can handle the situation two ways: let it be, or retaliate. It's a logical conclusion that Terrence's death was somehow related to his terrorizing the Wilshire citizenry. And even if that's not true, a lot of the Rangers' competition is going to think so. And, to Poppa, the Rangers' reputation is more important than his brother *or* the truth behind his killing. The Rangers' ability to intimidate is money in the bank.

"I hear that Williams is planning to raise the value of Rangers' stock before it has a chance to take a beating."

"What do you mean?" asked Brett.

"Just that it will continue to be rough, maybe rougher, for a little while on the streets. A message needs to be sent to the Wilshire district and to the Rangers' competition that the Rangers cannot be intimidated and that if one soldier falls, two will take his place. You get the picture?"

"Doesn't sound too good," said White sipping his beer and looking at Brett.

"What do you suggest?" asked Clark.

"We've talked about a neighborhood watch program for a long time. Now might be a good time to start."

"What exactly do you mean by a neighborhood watch program?" asked White.

"Well, there's the four of us for starters. We could patrol in twos, and use walkie-talkies. We could react fast to trouble."

"How fast?" said Clark. "It doesn't take long to kill a guy. Look what happened to Terrence Williams last night. The guy was just going to the john. If the Rangers are going to make an example of somebody, they're going to do it. And, excuse me if this sounds a little yellow, but I sure as hell don't want that somebody to be me."

There was silence for a moment before Sid White spoke. "Then what do *you* suggest, Jerry?"

"I don't know."

"We can all just store up food and hibernate until the Rangers say we can come out, White said, not in anger or to rebuff his friend, for he knew Clark was a brave man. Rather he was trying to make a point.

"Hell, I don't know," said Clark disgustedly.

"I just can't help but feel we've got to do something," said White. "You and I, Jerry, give these self-defense classes. We can take care of ourselves better than most of our friends. They look up to us. We give them hope and confidence."

"A lot of times we're lying to them, Sid, and you know it."

"But at least they live a few more minutes without fear. If they saw fear in our eyes, they'd go to pieces."

"But I *am* afraid, Sid. A smart person recognizes a tough spot when he sees one and doesn't go around trying to play John Wayne." Clark set his beer down, got up and walked around the room. "I'm sorry, Sid, but that's the way I feel."

"Hell, I'm scared, too, Jerry. I admit it. But I haven't

lived my life, spent my career in the Navy during the war fighting for a way of life only to surrender it to punk kid criminals who try to tell me how to live. I've fought for what I've got and there's no sense living any longer if it's all gone. You know what I mean, Jerry? I'm not playing the hero. And I'm scared, just like you. But I'm just as proud as I am scared and I'll be damned if they're going to step all over me."

Clark turned to his friend and smiled. "You're right, Sid. Dammit, you're right."

"You got the walkie-talkies, Ollie?" said White.

"In my car. Two of them."

"Okay. I'll take a watch tonight. How 'bout the rest of you?"

"I'll go with you, Sid," said Brett.

"Okay, then you and I will be the other team," said Neal to Clark.

"Good," said White. "Ollie go get those walkie-talkies and let's get down to business."

Neal left the room, came back a few minutes later, laid the radio devices on the coffee table and the four men planned their strategy.

It was about eight o'clock by the time Brett and Sid White parked at the corner of La Brea and Wilshire and started their patrol. It was dark and cold, about fifty degrees. Both men were wearing jackets. The only movements on the streets besides cars driving past were the two figures patrolling the street.

They turned down Kramer Street and walked over one block, turned left and came back up Cherry to Wilshire. Up and down the streets they went looking for anything out of the ordinary, any shadows or noises that shouldn't be there.

"How ya doin?" asked Brett.

"Fine. I'm a little chilly. How 'bout you?"

"Fine. You're a brave man, Sid, and I admire you for it."

"Hell, I'm scared, just like Jerry and you know it."

"Who said brave people aren't scared?"

White started to say something, then just smiled. "You're right. You gotta be pretty stupid not to be scared when you know the odds are against you and your life is threatened."

"That's right. It's what you do *after* that feeling that makes you brave or—"

"Yeah. Hey, you know maybe Ollie was wrong. Poppa might not retaliate against us. I mean, it's just Ollie's opinion."

"That's true," said Brett. "But you've got to admit, it makes a lot of sense. I think we're doing the right thing."

"You know something?"

"What?"

"I'm glad *you're* with me. It makes me feel a lot safer."

Brett just laughed.

Just then the walkie-talkie crackled to life. "Help!" a voice was saying. "Help! 1415 Atlas. 1415 Atlas!"

"Shit!" yelled White. "Follow me. It's two blocks away."

White and Brett ran full out down the street across Wilshire and down to Atlas. From the corner they could see movement and hear a commotion. They ran toward it. By the time they were twenty yards away, Brett could see Clark down on the sidewalk and three blacks beating Neal.

Brett yelled at the top of his lungs and got their attention. They dropped Neal's body and it fell like a sack of grain on the sidewalk a few feet from Clark. Instead of running, the youths turned to fight.

White tackled one of the men like a linebacker hitting a quarterback and they tumbled onto a nearby lawn. The sight of his friends lying bleeding on the cement had given White a strength and passion beyond his normal range. Brett grabbed one assailant and broke his elbow backwards across his knee. He was careful not to perform any seemingly superhuman feats which could connect him to the killing of Terrence White. He used standard, but highly effective, karate techniques. As the one assailant hit the ground screaming and looking at his arm in its unnatural position, Brett greeted the second with a kick to the solar plexus that left the man in a ball on the street gasping for air. Brett then delivered a kick to the man's rib cage that he knew would break several ribs and collapse his left lung.

Meanwhile, White had his man under control and, in fact, was beating the shit out of him. Brett pulled him off the unconscious man whose head rolled lifelessly to one side as White got to his feet.

"Let's call the police," said Brett.

"And an ambulance," said White looking at his wounded comrades lying on the ground.

"Dammit! Dammit! Why couldn't it have been us. Shit!" cried White.

Brett sent White to a nearby house to use the phone. A man who had apparently been watching what was going on from his window, opened his door and let White in.

White reported the incident and went back out to help Brett guard their captives. The guy White had taken on was still unconscious. The man Brett had kicked in the stomach was still down, but the third man, the one with the broken arm, had fled. White was too tired to go after him and Brett just let him go.

"You okay?" Brett said to White who was now kneeling beside Ollie who was bleeding from the head.

"Hell, I'm okay, but Ollie and Jerry look like they're hurt bad."

"Look, I'll talk fast. There's not much time. The police will be here any second."

"Good."

"That's not *good* for me," said Brett firmly, looking White hard in the eyes.

At first White didn't understand what Brett was getting at, then he got it. *No questions.* Brett had earned that much. And more, thought White. Without him, he and his two buddies would all be dead.

"Okay. Then get the hell outta here. I'll stop by your place when I get back from the hospital."

"See you later," said Brett. Then he was off like a flying shadow into the night.

Brett watched the eleven o'clock news and there *was* a brief item about the incident, but the commentator said details were "sketchy at this time."

Brett hoped some of those details would remain sketchy.

When he heard a knock at his door it was about twelve-thirty in the morning. He opened the door and ushered a weary Sid White into the living room. He had news, and it looked as though some of it was bad. Brett decided to just let White tell the tale.

"Drink?" said Brett.

"Vodka. A double," said White collapsing in a rust-colored chair opposite the couch and the balcony which looked out upon some rooftops and a shorter part of the L.A. skyline. It was a clear night, but White's mind was anything but lucid. He was a man in pain, but it wasn't his body that hurt.

"Here," said Brett handing White a stiff drink of Absolut and sitting down on the couch with one himself.

"Thanks," said the older man. He took a couple of full swallows and soon seemed less tense.

Still, Brett didn't ask any questions. He knew he'd be told everything, but White looked like an emotional minefield and Brett didn't know where the dynamite was buried.

"Ollie's dead," said White finally. Brett could see White's eyes awash in suppressed pain, hurt.

"Jesus, I'm sorry, Sid. I can't help but feel some of this is my fault."

"Don't ever say that again," said Sid sitting up straight and raising his chin. "Ollie, Jerry, and me are grown men and we knew what we were getting into. Ollie died for something any man would be proud to have died for—he was protecting his rights and property and the rights and property of his neighbors from criminals. From filth. By God," White's voice cracked with emotion, "he was a brave goddamned son-of-a-bitch who did *not* die in vain. And I'm one proud bastard that that son-of-a-bitch was my *very* good friend." White set his drink down, cradled his face in his hands and began to weep.

Brett got up and walked out onto the balcony and looked out upon the city, the battleground. Like all cities nowadays, thought Brett. *How in the hell did we get to this place?*

Brett sipped on his vodka and stood bent over the balcony railing for a while thinking about Ollie, a guy who he'd just had lunch with—who was in some morgue or mortuary right now. Brett wondered what happened to people when they die.

He raised a silent toast to Ollie and wished him Godspeed. After about ten minutes White joined Brett on the balcony.

"Sorry," said White.

"Nothing to be sorry about, Sid," said Brett still looking out upon the buildings.

"You want to know what else happened?"

"If you want to tell me."

"Jerry's going to be all right. He's got a concussion and a broken wrist. He'll be out of the hospital tomorrow or in a couple days."

"The cops arrived just as you were disappearing. They took the two downtown and booked them. One of the guys kept going on about 'another guy' who left."

"Me?"

"You. But Jerry was out by the time we got there so he didn't see you. And the cops didn't seem too interested in hearing about a guy who got away, especially since I said it was just the three of us."

"What about the guy who let you use his phone?"

"No problem. I talked with him and he wasn't sure who was fighting and who wasn't. Also, he wasn't too eager to talk with police for fear of getting his name in the papers. He was afraid the Rangers would come after *him*."

"So I'm in the clear."

"Yeah."

"What about you and Jerry?"

"What about us?"

"You're pressing charges?"

"Ollie was murdered. Nobody has to press charges. Jerry and I will be witnesses, but that won't be for a while. The wheels of justice grind pretty slowly, as I'm sure you know."

"If they grind at all."

"Right. So we've got some time before our numbers come up."

"Kind of a pessimistic way to look at it," said Brett turning to face White.

"It's gonna be a bitch, but I'm not afraid. And I know Jerry feels the same way."

The two were silent for a few moments. The ebbing tide of early morning traffic noises, the hum of the city, played softly in the background as the two friends stood contemplating life and death in a world gone mad.

White soon left and Brett sat alone on his couch trying to think of a solution.

The trouble had been there long before Brett appeared

on the scene. But it *was* true that he had started it in a different direction, accelerated it in some ways, right at his friends.

It was not self-recrimination he sought tonight, but a solution. Because even though Clark and White would try to be brave in the face of the trouble they were bound to encounter by being witnesses against the Rangers, there *would be* trouble, threats and, quite possibly, death for the two.

Ollie Neal had said it when asked how to finally stop the Rangers. There was only one way: take out Poppa Williams and Angelo Bandini. He also said it would be easier to assassinate the President of the United States.

But taking out Williams and Bandini, thought Brett, was now the goal.

Chapter 18

Brett awoke about seven the next morning and read the account of what had gone down the night before in the Wilshire district. The important thing, to Brett, was that there was no mention of a fourth member of the crime-watch patrol.

Although the article didn't come right out and say it, between the lines it intimated that the witnesses could be in for a rough time since other witnesses testifying against the Rangers had met with physical harassment and, at least in one case, death.

Brett knew he needed to act quickly and decisively, before the Rangers had time to put pressure on White and Clark. Therefore, Brett would have to orient himself to a new timetable. Action, not thought, was demanded and, thus, the risk factor would necessarily increase.

"Did I wake you?" said Brett into the phone.

"Not yet," said a female voice groggily. "It's only ten-thirty. Who is this? Whoever it is, you can't know me too well."

"Sorry Patty, maybe I should call back."

"Brett?" said the young woman, now alert. "Is that you?"

"Yes. Hey, I didn't think you'd . . ."

"No problem. I was supposed to get up shortly anyhow. What's going on?"

"Well, I've got some bad news I'm afraid."

"What?" she said, her voice indicating an almost instant alertness.

"It's Ollie Neal and Jerry Clark, Sid's buddies."

"Oh my God!"

"Ollie's been killed."

"Oh no!" she cried. "And Jerry?"

"He got a concussion and he's in the hospital. But he'll be okay. Sid's okay, too, but he's pretty broken up about Ollie."

"Oh, this is just terrible. I feel so sad. Ollie was such a nice guy. Jerry, too. Even if he did come on to me a little too much. Oh, I just feel sick about all this. I'll have to stop down and see Sid."

"Yeah, I'm sure he'd appreciate it. I'd like to see you, Patty. Today."

"Yeah, sure. Socially, or is this business?"

"What kind of business could I have with you?"

"I don't know, you sound a little upset, like you have something important to tell me."

"It's important. But only to me. How about lunch?"

"Okay. Give me some time, though, okay?"

"Twelve-thirty?"

"One o'clock."

"See you then," said Brett and hung up.

"I really like this place for lunch," said Patty as they were seated under an overhanging willow tree. Butterfields was located on a hill just off Sunset near the Sunset Strip. Although there were dining facilities inside where most tables had a view of a large stone fireplace, the outside tables, on a warm Southern California afternoon, were the perfect backdrop for a pleasant lunch. It made Brett feel as though he should be talking about a movie deal rather than asking Patty for help.

"What's good here?" he asked.

"The spinach salad is about the only thing I ever order. But then I usually eat a light lunch."

Brett ordered two spinach salads and a carafe of a good California chenin blanc.

"I called Sid after we talked," said Patty after the food and wine were delivered.

"How's he taking it?" asked Brett, not indicating he had seen the man earlier that morning.

"He's pretty shaken up. It's just awful. All the victims in the past and now Ollie and Jerry."

"Yeah, I know. What kind of people would do something like that?" Brett watched her face for a reaction. She glanced down and seemed to seek out answers in her wine glass, but said nothing.

"You know anybody like that?" said Brett.

She looked up at him and his eyes met hers. She knew he was not just speaking rhetorically. She looked away and started toying with her salad.

"What do you think of people who do things like that?"

"Are you getting at something?" she finally said, dropping her fork and looking up at Brett.

"Yes, I am. But I want to know how you feel about something first."

"About what?"

"About what I just asked you. How do you feel about people who do things like what happened to Ollie and Jerry last night?"

"How do you think I feel?"

"I really don't know. I want to hear it from your own lips and see how it looks in your eyes when you say it."

"I hate it, okay? You satisfied? What did you expect me to say? That I like people who go around beating up and killing my friends?"

"I don't know. Would you continue to associate with those people if you knew they were killers?"

Patty picked up her purse and started to get up, but Brett grabbed her firmly by the forearm. She felt the strength in his grip and her resistance drained from her body.

"Would you associate with the killers of your friends?"

"No. You satisfied?"

"Not quite."

"Hey, let's cut the crap and get to the bottom line. What do you want from me?" Patty was used to getting to the bottom line. She was a tough lady and some survival instinct had just risen to the surface.

"Okay. I saw you the other night in the Brass Ball."

"So?"

"In the same room with Angelo Bandini."

"Shit!" she said and relaxed back in her chair. "So what do you think that means?"

"You have an in with the Rangers."

"That's a laugh and a half. That's like saying the Christians had an in with the Roman Emperor."

"Explain it to me. Please."

"Why the hell should I?"

"Because it might save Sid and Jerry's lives."

"Says who?"

"Look, stop trying to fence me in. I'm not bargaining for a trick, I'm trying to keep Sid and Jerry from getting murdered. You can help or you can walk. It's as simple as that."

Patty mellowed a little. "I don't know what the hell you're up to, but . . ."

The two sat in silence for a few moments as Patty sipped her wine and Brett toyed with his salad. She seemed to be going over her options and the consequences of each. Finally she took a deep breath and said, "Okay. What do you want to know?"

"What is your relationship with Angelo Bandini?"

"He's a friend," she said turning her head and looking absently toward another table.

"Anything more than that?"

"Why don't you just come right out and say it, Brett," she said turning back to him angrily. "You want to know if he's my pimp? If he drives me around to street corners and wears a big hat while I go upstairs and screw some guy?"

"I don't think that's the case. But rather than guess, I'd like to just hear you say it."

Patty looked down at her plate.

"I'm not trying to humiliate you, Patty," said Brett putting his hand on hers.

"You know this isn't any 'What's a nice girl like me doing in a place like this' scene. I don't really mind what I do. It's not forever. The money's good and I'm not on the street. I used to work for the phone company. But I like to dress well—I mean really well—I like to drive a nice car, live in a nice place, and not owe it to some guy who thinks he owns my butt, just because we got the same last name."

"Not everyone fed up with working for the phone company decides to be a hooker. How did it happen?"

Patty took a deep breath, opened her purse, took out a dark-colored cigarette and lit it. "I used to make the party rounds with some of the hotshots at the phone company. You know the scene—the execs size up the secretarial talent and well, you know. So—and I'm not bragging—I was an all-star, if you know what I mean; guys liked to have me on their arms. I was like a 'designer-label' date."

"I get the picture," said Brett pouring himself more wine.

"So, anyhow I would circulate at these parties and I'd meet a lot of guys that way. One night I met this woman who was with the guy whose house the party was at. Great place. In the Hollywood Hills. The whole deal.

"So this lady and I start talking and we strike up a friendship. We meet a couple of times for lunch and then she sits me down at her place and has this heart-to-heart talk with me. There she is living in this great penthouse overlooking the Sunset Strip and I'm thinking she probably inherited money or divorced some guy who was loaded. But then she drops this bombshell—she tell's me she's a hooker. Not a street hooker or anything, but still a hooker. Instead of making twenty-five dollars a pop on the street corner and screwing a dozen guys a night, she makes anywhere from three hundred to a thousand dollars a night with just one guy. And, of course, you can make more when certain people come to town, but I was never much for the kinky scene.

"Anyhow, I got involved in the scene. There were a lot of parties in those days; that was a few years ago. At one of the parties I met Angelo Bandini. He'd just gotten out of prison, but I didn't know that till later. He's a good-looking guy and he has this charisma. He's got the feel of power.

"So we became friends and lovers. But for him I didn't charge, you know. We actually dug each other a lot.

"A few months later our relationship cooled off, but we stayed in touch. Then I had a real bad thing happen to me. It's not necessary to go into details, but some guy turned on me and I almost got killed. As it was, I was in the hospital for a couple weeks. While I was in there, Angie came to see me and we renewed our relationship, on a romantic basis.

"But then, after a while it cooled again. He knew I was running out of money and that I wasn't real thrilled about being supported exclusively by him if we weren't actually together, you know what I mean. So he said I could go to work for him and that his people would give me all the protection I'd need. And he'd make sure I wouldn't get any weirdos like the one who put me in the hospital.

"So I've been working out of Angie's stable, so to speak, for about a year now."

"And he's treated you well?"

"I didn't say that, did I?" she said with some passion.

"No. So how has he treated you?"

"Like shit, if you really want to know."

"Then why don't you get out?"

"Two reasons. First, economics. Second, Angie doesn't take it too well when people leave him. I'm last year's news to Angie now. If you're female and over twenty-five in this town you're about ready for the old folks home. There's a couple girls hanging around now who aren't old enough to get into an R-rated film by themselves."

"So why doesn't he let you go?"

"He will, eventually. Right now I'm used for second and third-rate business people he wants to impress. You know, a snap of the finger and some babe drops her drawers. It's very impressive to a lot of guys. But the guys he really tries to impress get the jailbait and the girls who *really* are willing to please. For them a doctor is always on standby."

"Sounds like a rough business."

"I don't need sympathy. I put myself exactly where I am. I'll get out somehow. There are people who got it worse.

"Now you heard my life story. What do you want to know about Angie for?"

"I want to meet Angie and Poppa," said Brett simply.

Patty laughed. "Oh yeah? You got a death wish or something?"

"No. Take me seriously, Patty. I know you have no reason to believe this, but I know what I'm doing."

"I don't believe you. But even if I did, the only way to meet Angie and Poppa is to give them reason to believe you got something they want."

"And what do they want?"

"Money and power."

"How do they make their money?"

"Lots of it comes from selling drugs."

"How would I go about making contact?"

"You get word to them through proper channels."

"Are you a proper channel?"

"Not me. I don't want to die. I'll get out somehow, but when I go it won't be in a box. No sir, no thanks."

"I need an in and I need it fast, Patty."

"But I have a feeling you're not going to be bringing them glad tidings. And you know what they do to the messenger who brings the bad news."

"How else could I get in?"

"I don't know."

"Look Patty, I'm serious," Brett said firmly.

"Just because you're serious doesn't make it any the less stupid."

"I need your help, Patty. I'll do it without you, but my chances are a lot better if you help me."

She sensed his mood change and she looked him in the eye. "What exactly do you want to get close to Angie and Poppa for?"

"I can't tell you."

"Can I guess?"

"I think it's rather obvious."

"You're right. It is obvious. But the thing you don't think *is* so obvious, which I *do*, is that you're just committing suicide. Nobody can go against Angie and Poppa and come out alive. Hey, I think it's great you feel such loyalty to Sid and the other guys, but don't be an idiot."

"Okay, so I understand your point of view."

"What exactly would you want me to do anyhow?"

"I've got to get close to Angie and Poppa. Anything that accomplishes that will help."

"You're crazy."

"Does that mean you won't help?"

"Let's not put it that way. Let's just say, I like you and I don't want to see you hurt. Let's leave it at that, okay?" she said finishing her wine and stubbing out her cigarette.

Brett paid the tab and he and Patty left Butterfields.

Chapter 19

Brett dropped Patty off at the apartment building and drove over to the hospital to see Jerry Clark.

"Brett," said Sid getting up from his chair next to Clark's bed. "Glad to see you. Here's a chair," he said swinging another chair from the corner of the room around so that it was next to the bed facing Clark.

"How you doing?" said Brett to the man in the bed.

Clark's head was bandaged. Part of the bed was raised so that he was almost sitting up facing his friends. He looked tired, but in good spirits.

"Okay, I guess," he said smiling. "Probably'd be dead now if it weren't for Sid here. Some martial arts self-defense instructor I turned out to be! But hell, I'm alive, right? Ollie looked real bad. Real bad. I thought he might be dead. Lucky bastard."

Brett looked at White and the ex-Navy man gave him a sharp look. Obviously he hadn't told Clark that Neal was dead. It made sense under the circumstances. He'd find out soon enough.

"So how long you in for?" said Brett sitting down in the chair.

"A day or two. Just for observation. Or so they tell me. Nothing serious. Coulda got the same damn thing falling down the stairs or slipping getting out of the Jacuzzi. No big deal. I'm trying to think of what I'm going to tell our Tuesday night self-defense class about how to take care of themselves on the street."

"Look Jerry," said Brett firmly enough to get the older man's attention. "You were out there as their first line of defense. You were out there protecting them. You don't condemn your army because they get wounded defending you. Don't worry about it. If anything, you're going to be a hero to them."

Clark thought about that a moment and finally said, "You know, the kid's right, Sid. You and Ollie and I are kinda like heroes at that. I just wish we would have won, that's all."

"It's a long war out there on the streets," said Sid. "It'll be a while before we know who really won."

The three men talked for about an hour until a nurse came in and told Brett and Sid that visiting hours were over. They said their good-byes and left.

"Need a ride?"

"No thanks, son. I drove over. Wouldn't mind sharin' some coffee with you, though."

Brett understood that Sid wanted to tell Brett something and was taking his own time about it.

The coffee shop was across the street from the hospital. There was about an equal smattering of hospital-smocked personnel, students from a nearby high school, and people who looked to be either just passing by or visiting friends and relatives in the hospital.

"I thought it was best not to tell Jerry about Ollie yet."

"Sounds logical. What did the doctors say?"

"They recommended it. At least until they can determine the extent of Jerry's injury. Dammit! It's all such a mess."

"Something else going on I don't know about, Sid?"

The older man sighed deeply as their coffee was set in front of them. White played with the cup, moving it around in the saucer. Yeah. There's somethin' else."

"What?"

"I talked with a guy who came by to see Jerry this morning. He's a guy Jerry used to work with on the force. It seems the cops spotted a couple of Rangers posing as orderlies earlier today. It's obvious what they were planning to do. Jerry and I are the witnesses who can send those two guys to jail for a long time."

"So what are you going to do?"

"They doubled the guards on the floor. Some of the guards are undercover, dressed like doctors or nurses. They feel they owe it to one of their own."

"What about you?"

"Good question." Sid sipped his coffee.

"I'm scared, Brett. Scared as hell." White put his hand to his forehead and massaged his temples. His head was bowed as if he had made an embarrassing admission.

"That's nothing to be ashamed of, Sid."

"But I don't know what the hell I'm gonna do. I can't leave town and as sure as I'm sittin' here, if I stay I'm a dead man. And I'm not saying this in order for you to look out for me. That'd be great, but you can't watch me forever. No, it's just that I'm in one hell of a spot."

There wasn't much Brett could say. But then White didn't want a pep talk. He needed somebody to talk to—a person who would grasp and understand what he had to say.

Brett went back to the apartment and fixed himself some espresso. Since Patty wouldn't help him, and now that Sid and Jerry were in imminent danger, Brett's position was becoming even more exasperating.

He read the afternoon paper and there was a more detailed account of what had happened last night on Atlas street. Still, there was no mention of a fourth crime-watch member. Although the account was more detailed than that in the morning paper, the story was buried further back in the paper—on page twenty-six.

It was a tragedy of major proportions to the residents of the Wilshire district, but already old news to the rest of the city.

Brett was fixing dinner about six-thirty when he heard a pounding on his door.

He opened it and Patty rushed in. She threw her arms around Brett's neck and started to cry.

"What's wrong, Patty? Tell me! What's wrong?" He guided the distraught young woman to his couch and sat down beside her.

"It's Sid," she cried through her tears.

"Oh my God," said Brett. "Tell me!"

"I called Sid after you and I got back from lunch. He

wasn't in, but I got hold of him about three-thirty. He said he was tired and wanted to take a nap. I suggested we go out to dinner and he agreed. I went down to his place about five-thirty and we had a drink. We left shortly after that and were just on our way to Shiny's for dinner and—"

"And what?"

"We were walking along and this car pulls up and knocks me down and grabs Sid. They slapped him around a little and stuffed him into the back seat and sped off."

"Oh shit!" exclaimed Brett.

"And another thing," she said.

"What?"

"I recognized the car and the guy driving."

Brett looked at her intensely.

"He works for Angie."

"Did he see you?"

"I can't be sure, but I don't think so. They didn't have any reason to think I'd be with him. They don't know a great deal about my social life. They don't care really as long as I do my job."

"Did you call the police?"

"No."

"Go back to your place and call them. Then come down here after they've gone and I'll be ready."

"For what?"

"You're going to introduce me to Angie," said Brett firmly.

"But how?"

"You'll tell me when you come back down."

"But Brett—" she started to argue.

"There's not going to be any argument about this Patty. I'm Sid's—and probably Jerry's—only chance. I've got to act immediately. I'll let you off the hook, but you're going to get me in. Understand?"

Reluctantly, but resignedly, she said "Okay."

"Now get up to your apartment and call the police."

Patty left and Brett looked through his wardrobe for a conservative suit.

"So what's the plan?" said Brett when she came back down about an hour and a half later dressed in a somewhat startling white dress you could see through if the light hit it right.

"I'm going to introduce you as a guy I met at a party a few years back who I just happened to run into again at a Beverly Hills restaurant. You've got a lot of money and are interested in making more. You don't like the low and slow pay of the banks and you're looking for something a little more lucrative and exciting to put your money into."

"Sounds reasonable."

"From there you're on your own."

"And you're in the clear. You won't be responsible for my behavior."

"That's right. Remember, Angie's no dummy. He's not going to show any cards until he knows you better."

"I'm not asking him to play cards."

"Yeah, I know," she said. "You gotta drink?"

"Sure. Absolut okay?"

"Perfect. Make it a double."

"You got it," Brett said and went into the kitchen.

"I'm scared, Brett," Patty said loud enough so that Brett could hear her in the kitchen.

"Look, you're not responsible for what I do after you deliver me—and introduce me. I'm just an old friend who's got some money—as far as you know. You just bought my line. Believe me, nobody's going to be able to find me after this is over," said Brett walking back into the room with her glass of vodka.

"After what's over?"

"You'll see," he said handing her her drink.

"I wouldn't even be doing this if it weren't for Sid. I mean, I know the guy and well—Jesus—I just couldn't live with myself if I didn't at least do *something*. You know?"

"Yes, I know. What am I going to be in for tonight? Prepare me a little."

"All right. Hey, you're not going to go in there guns blazing, or nothin' like that, are you?"

"No. I just want to meet Angie and then I'll take it from there. Fair enough?"

"Okay. Well, there's a party tonight at Angie's. No big deal. There's a party there most every night. Several of us are supposed to bring guests, guys with money."

"Great. Sounds simple then."

"That part is. Angie's lived his life among cons and he can't be conned easily. You know?"

"Okay. How about the way I'm dressed?"

"Looks like money to me. You know, it's a funny thing about you."

"What's that?"

"You never said different, but, just in case you think I'm *real* dumb, you don't look like any engineer I ever knew. And you keep pretty loose hours."

"You're right."

"About what?"

"I keep loose hours."

"In other words," she said, "mind my own business."

"That's right," said Brett. "What about Poppa Williams? Will he be at the party tonight?"

"Probably not. But he might be. Never know with Poppa."

"You know him?"

"A little," she said taking a long sip of her drink. "But I know Angie a lot better."

"What's Poppa like?"

"Big guy. Lots of muscles. Real dangerous, from what I can tell. First time I ever met him I was with Angie—when things were real good between him and me—and we went to this party up in the hills—Encino, I think—and well, anyhow, this guy, the host, Bob or something like that, was glad-handing everybody. Angie and Poppa were dressed to kill and smiling and having a grand old time. Poppa and this guy were real buddy-buddy. Hell, I woulda thought they were school chums or somethin', if I didn't know Poppa never went to school. Anyhow, everything's real cool and so the evening goes along smoothly, Poppa and this guy shake hands and say good night. Poppa, his date, and Angie and I get into this limo and Poppa in a real calm, cool voice tells Angie, 'Kill him.' Can you believe that? 'Kill him.' I just about died. Naturally I didn't say anything, you know, but it was like out of 'The Godfather' or somethin'. Weird. The guy's a mean dude."

Brett digested the information and polished off his drink. "Thanks for telling me. Anything else of use you can tell me?"

"I don't know. Just be careful. Angie and Poppa get a lot of mileage out of intimidation, but their reputation as tough guys is well-deserved. Every now and then, just to keep up appearances, they get a little rough. And if anybody crosses them, especially so that other people notice it, that person is as good as dead. You get my drift?"

"Yes. So you about ready to go?"

"Let me just freshen up a sec."

"Sure," said Brett getting up. "The bathroom's down the hall."

"I'll find it," she said setting down her drink. Patty got up and disappeared through the doorway leading into the hall.

Brett walked out onto the balcony and looked out reflectively at the city. The night air was chilly. He knew he was the hunter and Williams and Bandini the prey. Brett felt the heightening of senses that hadn't registered so strongly since he left Japan. There hadn't been any reason for them to. Until now.

Chapter 20

Brett and Patty took her MG up into the hills to Angelo Bandini's house. As they drove up the tortuous roads leading to the stilt-supported house, the city fell further and further into the backdrop until it became a winking sea of lights.

Two tall jet black doors adorned with gold fixtures opened when Patty rang the lighted doorbell. A man in a white jacket ushered the couple inside. Straight ahead was a large white grand piano beyond which a wall of glass revealed the city's million lights flickering off and on. The view fit in with Bandini's opulence so well it seemed as though it were merely expensive wallpaper.

"Not bad, eh?" said Patty leading Brett to the bar which stood off to the left just in front of the large kitchen, which had an attractive array of hanging copper pots and wooden accessories.

"Sir?" said the man to Brett from across the bar.

Brett looked at the selection and felt certain Absolut would be among the choices. It was. He ordered for himself and Patty and then followed her out to the patio.

"How does he justify this to poverty-stricken members of the gang?" said Brett sipping at his vodka and taking in the view.

"Most followers don't know about it. And the ones that do either justify it as a business expense—to take money from the Gotbucks types—or, if they don't buy that, Bandini simply turns them on to a few of the pleasures."

"Like her," said Brett tilting his head in the direction of

a strawberry blond wearing a wrap-around skirt and a beige Danskin. The girl, who Brett figured to be about sixteen—at the most—was laughing, throwing her long mane back and intimately gesturing with, and touching, a couple of trendy business types who were enchanted with their companion.

"Yeah, like her. Like me sometimes," she said sighing.

"So where's the boss?"

"Angie? I don't see him around. But he's bound to be here somewhere. Probably doing some business or getting high in one of the bedrooms. Or getting laid. Who knows. He's around, though. Don't look anxious. Remember, Angie can see through most people like he was lookin' through glass. Be careful."

Brett and Patty mingled for a while and made small talk. Then they sat on a leather couch and watched a large-screen TV which was playing a videotape of the first Sugar Ray Leonard-Roberto Duran fight.

About a half hour later Patty nudged Brett and said, "There he is."

Brett recognized Bandini from the night he saw him in the Brass Ball. He was tanned and dressed in white slacks, a shirt open to the middle of his hairy chest and draped in gold around his wrists and neck. He was smiling and had his arm around an older man, an Oriental, who was impeccably, if traditionally, dressed in a blue tailored suit. Bandini whispered something into the Oriental's ear. They both laughed and shook hands. Bandini raised his hand and waved a young girl over who snuggled up to the older man and the odd couple disappeared back into a bedroom.

Bandini made his way out into the living room where he was warmly greeted by his guests.

"Ready?" Patty said to Brett.

"Not yet."

"What's wrong?"

"You've got to settle down," he said coolly.

"What do you mean?"

"You say Bandini can read people like books. Lighten up. You're breathing fast, your heart's beating fast and making one of your cute little—or not so little—breasts look like its dancing."

"You're right," she said and sat back on the couch.

"Calm yourself. Don't worry. You're off the hook after you introduce me. None of this will get back to you. You met me at a party years ago, and thought I was a nice guy. You saw me at a restaurant a few nights ago, still with no reason to think I was lying, knew about the party, and wanted to put me in touch with Bandini. You thought you were doing the Italian a big favor and nobody can prove differently."

"But what if they make you talk?"

"That won't happen. Trust me. No matter what."

"What if they trace you back to my apartment building?"

"This isn't going to take much time. By the time any checking is done, if in fact it *is* done, I'll be long gone. Besides, I've got something that will make them less likely to do a big research job on me."

"And that is?"

"Money."

"Look Brett, we're not talking about a few thousand dollars here."

"Neither am I. Don't worry. I know what I'm doing. Trust me."

"You ready now?"

"You?"

Patty heaved a large sigh, seeming to relieve some tension. "Ready as I'll ever be," she said getting up.

Bandini was slowly making his way toward the couch beside which Brett and Patty were now standing.

"One more thing," said Brett.

"Yeah?"

"Keep an eye out for the driver who snatched Sid."

"Okay."

"Patty, honey, how are you?" Angie said putting his arm around her and kissing her on the cheek.

"Fine, Angie. There's someone I'd like you to meet," she said turning to Brett.

"Angie Bandini," said the Italian, firmly gripping Brett's hand and smiling widely.

"Brett Alexander. Pleased to meet you. Nice place you got here."

"I like it. Great place to entertain. You got an armful

with this one," Bandini said tilting his head toward Patty and slapping Brett on the shoulder.

"I wonder if we might have a little talk when you have a free moment?" said Brett.

Bandini stopped and though his smile remained in gear, Brett could tell that Bandini's senses were now turned on.

"Sure, sure. Give me a few minutes and we can have a chat. Just a few minutes, eh?" After kissing Patty on the cheek once, Bandini was off again working his way through his social gauntlet.

"What do you think?" said Brett to Patty once Bandini was out of hearing range.

"Hard to tell. He's meeting with you. You'll know soon enough." They both returned to their seats and continued to watch the fight.

About the twelfth round a short, powerfully built man came up to Brett and introduced himself.

"Mr. Alexander?"

"Yes."

"My name is Cal. Mr. Bandini will see you now. Please follow me."

Brett excused himself from Patty and followed Cal into Bandini's office. Cal left and closed the door behind him. Bandini was on the phone and held up one finger to indicate he wouldn't be long.

Soon Bandini hung up the phone, stood, reached across his desk and shook Brett's hand.

"Mr. Alexander, welcome," said Bandini seating himself behind his desk again. "You said something about business. I didn't catch your line."

"I buy and sell," said Brett, taking a seat in front of the desk.

Bandini smiled and said, "I see. That doesn't tell me much. How can I be of assistance to you?"

"Let's put it this way. I've got a great deal of money and I don't like the kind of interest banks pay."

"So you look at me as some kind of investment counselor?" said Bandini taking a cigarette from a box on his desk and offering the box to Brett. Brett declined.

"Not exactly. I look at you, and Poppa of course, as the biggest dope peddlers in the city; or at least as two of the ones with the biggest aspirations. I think we could help each other."

"I don't know where you got your information, Mr. uh, Alexander, but I think it could use some rechecking."

"I don't think so. I don't make grandstand plays. I know what I'm saying or I don't say it. I'm a rich man and I didn't get that way being stupid. You and Poppa are smart, too. I do my homework and, believe me, the idea didn't just come to me on the spur of the moment in your living room."

Bandini didn't say anything for a moment.

Brett raised his eyebrows as if to say, "Oh well," and started to get up. He said, "Like I said, I do my homework. There are other players in the game who I'm sure would be interested."

"Sit down, there's no hurry. How do you know Patty?" said Bandini noncommittally.

"Patty. Patty's not important. She's some over-the-hill piece of ass. She thinks she ran into me by accident at a restaurant the other night. I wanted to meet with you, casually. I found out about the party and made Patty my invitation."

"You know," said Bandini lighting his cigarette as he spoke. "A lot of two-bit operators make silly plays like this all the time."

"Ever hear the phrase 'money talks?' "

Bandini smiled. "Once or twice."

"We could beat around the bush all night long. Call my bluff or show me the door," said Brett looking Bandini hard in the eye.

"I like you, Alexander. I really do. Not too many people talk like that to me."

"And get away with it, I know. Look, do we deal?"

"How much you want to . . . invest?"

"What would make your operation start to hum?"

"Cash?"

"Cash."

"How about a million five?"

"How about three?"

Bandini smiled widely again. "You know, that's a pretty impressive figure. But then . . ."

"But what?"

"Anybody can *say* the word million."

"So you want to see a little good faith money?"

"I'm sure you understand my position."

"I do. How about I bring a hundred thousand, cash, to our next meeting. That satisfy you?"

"I think we might be able to do business."

"Now that I've satisfied *your* requirements and, since you're a businessman, I'm sure you realize business isn't a one-way street."

"What's the catch?" Bandini's senses heightened to razor sharpness.

"No catch. I just want Williams to be there, too."

"Why? That's a little unusual."

"For one thing, I know you two are partners. Even though I'd be handing *you* the money, and you and he direct where it goes, what's done with it, we're *all* partners, then. Secondly, I've been following what's been going down in the Wilshire district. From what I hear from my sources downtown, it could go either way. Williams is pressing his luck. I'm not about to put my money on a horse that's going to pull up lame down the stretch. Like I said, I didn't make my money being stupid; or by trusting people with my money who I don't have a personal take on."

Bandini stubbed out his cigarette.

"I'll get back to you, okay?"

"Call him tonight. I'll mill around. We don't have to meet tonight, but let's set it up. Nice doing business with you, Angie," said Brett getting up.

"We haven't done any business, Mr. Alexander. I haven't admitted that anything you said was true. However, you are right that Mr. Williams and I are businessmen and any time another businessman comes to us with a proposal involving millions of dollars, I feel obliged to inform him of that proposal. That's all. As for reaching Mr. Williams tonight, I'll do my best to accommodate you. I'll have Cal tell you if I reach Mr. Williams later tonight."

"Thanks."

Bandini got up and showed Brett out.

Brett rejoined Patty in the living room and they went out onto the patio to talk.

"Well?"

"I think it went okay," said Brett. "But I won't know for a little while. You see the driver?"

"Yes. He came in just after you went in to meet with Angie. He's standing over next to the fireplace. He's the one wearing the brown sports coat."

"The bald guy?"

"Yeah. What now?"

"Go over and make some small talk with him. Say you remember seeing him at one of Angie's parties, whatever. Find out when he's going to leave. Then come back and let me know."

Brett watched Patty go through her paces with the bald man. She had a way about her that was hard for most guys to resist.

Brett went back out onto the patio to await Patty's return. About ten minutes later Patty joined Brett on the patio.

"He says he's working tonight."

"Probably guarding Sid."

"If he's still alive."

"No sense thinking otherwise. All we can do is go on the assumption he's alive and try to save him."

"He said he was just taking a break and that he'd be leaving in a few minutes."

"All right. I've got to talk to Cal for a second. Then I'm going to leave. Think you can get home without your car?"

"I don't think it'll be a problem getting a ride," she said sarcastically. "Just don't wreck my car."

"Give me your keys," he said. "I'll give you a call later." Patty took her car keys out of her purse and gave them to Brett.

"Good luck," she said to him as he turned and walked purposefully away.

"Cal," said Brett to Bandini's man.

"Mr. Alexander. What can I do for you?"

"Give Mr. Bandini a message for me."

"Certainly."

"Tell him that I have some pressing business elsewhere this evening and that I'll call him tomorrow. I *have* the number."

"I will give Mr. Bandini your message."

"Thanks," said Brett and left.

Outside, Brett walked to Patty's MG and scanned the neighborhood and the other parked cars for anyone who might be watching. He unlocked the door, got in, and slumped down in the seat to await the bald man's departure.

He didn't have to wait long. About fifteen minutes later, the fellow came walking down the driveway and out to a late-model Chevrolet, got in, and pulled away. Brett followed a moderate distance behind, without his lights at first, then with his lights on as they began to hit the more populated foothills below.

They hit Sunset at the bottom of the hill and the bald man turned left on Sunset and drove east for about two miles until he got to La Brea. Then he turned left and took the main street up to Franklin, turned right and took Franklin past Vine about a mile, parked just off Franklin on Grover and went into the right side of a duplex, looking around him for a tail as he disappeared inside the front door.

Brett continued on Franklin about a half a block, parked, and came back around to the corner of Grover and Franklin on foot. The duplex was white with green shutters around the windows. The second story was dark, but there were lights on in two front windows of the bottom story.

Brett crept up to and along the right side of the house, close to a window and overheard two men talking.

"Angie says to waste him," said the first man, the man Brett figured to be the bald man.

"Why didn't we just do that in the first place?" complained the second man.

"Angie changed his mind. As far as you're concerned, that's enough reason. Understand?"

"Okay, okay. No need to get touchy. So what's the plan?"

"No big deal. We just take old Sid for a ride out to Binny's boat and Binny'll take him for a long ride out in the Pacific, put a little weight in his shoes and that's the whole ballgame. He still out?"

"Like a light. For a while I thought we gave the old guy too much of that stuff. But he'll be all right. What's the use anyhow, right?"

"Go upstairs and bring him down. I'll call Binny and tell him to be ready."

"Okay," said the second man.

Brett heard footsteps getting further away. The second man had left the room. Brett figured that there were only two men in the house. At this point he had no options anyhow. He went around to the back of the duplex and found the door locked. Quickly he removed a tool from his pocket and picked the lock. Ninja training consisted of many arts, not all of them punching and kicking.

Once inside, Brett remained perfectly still. His senses were tingling antennae, gathering data and relaying it for analysis. There was movement upstairs and in the front room where Brett had heard the two voices. Other than that there was no sound.

The man in the front room was talking on the phone, as Brett could tell by hearing just one-way conversation. The bottom of the stairs was not visible from the front room and Brett moved to the steps and crept soundlessly up to the second floor. At the top of the stairs Brett heard sounds coming from a room down the hall, a room where a light was on, shining into the blackness of the dark hallway. Brett moved silently to the doorway and peered in. He saw Sid and another man. Sid was unconscious. The other man was trying to get Sid on his feet, but the old Navy man was not cooperating. The kidnapper's back was to Brett while he tried to pick up the heavy man and get him moving. Looking at the man's back, Brett made a decision. At that moment the man was as good as dead.

As quickly and silently as though he was walking in feather-soled shoes on shiny glass, Brett moved into the room. Grabbing the man by the head like a chiropractor getting ready to give an adjustment, Brett jerked and twisted the man's head and neck violently to one side, making a sharp snapping sound as he did.

Sid White's drugged and nearly lifeless body fell back into a chair as he slipped from the grasp of his kidnapper. Brett eased the dead man silently to the floor. Next he felt White's pulse and looked into his eyes. Convinced that White didn't need his immediate attention, Brett glided silently downstairs and took up a position just outside the front room where the bald man was still talking on the phone.

Brett made his move. He moved to the center of the archway leading into the front room and froze.

"Hi," said the man, holding a gun on Brett and putting down the phone. "You wondering how I knew you were there?"

"It crossed my mind," said Brett calmly.

"Reflection in the window," he said tilting his head in the direction of the window behind him. "If not for that, I'm sure I'd be dead by now. Right?"

Brett said nothing.

"Let's not drag this thing out. I'm not really interested in why you're here and I'm sure you're not in the mood to tell me, are you?"

"No."

"Then let's get this over with."

The man aimed the silencer-equipped gun at Brett and started closing his finger around the trigger. A bullet fired in Brett's direction, but he dived out of the way.

"That's not possible," said the man dumbfounded as Brett lay unharmed in a squatting position in the corner of the room. He had ducked, and come up on his feet. "No one could react that quickly."

The man fired again and again, but each time Brett dived and rolled safely away. By constantly watching the man's eyes and muscle reflexes, Brett was able to anticipate the direction of each shot. Finally the man ran out of bullets and threw the gun at Brett, who caught it and moved in close to the stunned man.

"Who the hell are you?" said the man, just before Brett hit him in the throat with his knuckles. The man gasped, his eyes bulged and he fell to the ground. The man would be dead in a matter of seconds.

Brett then went upstairs to revive Sid White. He looked into the eyes of the older man and then applied acupressure therapy on him, rubbing particular acupuncture points. Gradually White came around, blinking his eyes, disoriented, not knowing where he was. But he recognized Brett and that was a start.

With White's arm around his neck, Brett got the man

moving and took him out the back door and to an alley directly behind the duplex. He sat White down next to a garbage can and went to bring the car around to the alley and pick up White. Brett loaded White into the car and drove to a hotel over on Sunset where he checked in under an assumed name.

Brett quickly went over in his mind what had just happened. He couldn't afford a mistake, and he was certain he hadn't made any.

White made a moaning sound on the bed and was becoming more coherent.

"Where am I?" he asked through a haze of drugged disorientation.

"You're safe, Sid," said Brett going to his friend's side. "Just relax. You'll stay here for a while, until things are safe outside."

The older man was agreeable, but then he would have been agreeable to just about anything in his condition.

Brett made White lie back on the bed and rest, then used the phone next to the bed to call Patty.

"Hello?"

"Patty?"

"Yes," she said in a rather businesslike manner.

"You're not alone?"

"That's right."

"Just act naturally. Laugh a little."

Patty chuckled playfully and said, "Not right now, honey, I'm busy. But you know I want to see you."

"Good," said Brett. "Now listen to what I tell you. I got Sid out. There was trouble, but there were no traces that can lead back to you or me. You can count on it."

"That's wonderful," Patty said laughing again. "I can't wait to see you."

"You know where the Star Motel is on Sunset?"

"Sure do."

"Can you get here sometime tonight?"

"Probably."

"Come to room four. Knock four times if you're bringing trouble. Otherwise just knock twice. Understand?"

"Got it. Now you be a good boy till I see you tomorrow;

save some of that for me, you hear?" said Patty playing her part.

"Good girl," said Brett. "See you later."

Time went by slowly for Brett. Sid was out cold for the first couple hours, then gradually he began to regain consciousness. By two-thirty a.m. White was sitting up in bed drinking some coffee, dusting the cobwebs off his brain.

"It was the Rangers, wasn't it?" said White finally.

"Yeah. Patty recognized the driver of the car and identified him at a Rangers' party. Then I followed him to where they had you stashed and got you out."

"Got me out? You mean you . . ."

"I got you out, Sid. That's all there is to it," said Brett putting an end to that line of questioning.

"You say Patty identified the driver. I'm not sure I follow," said White sipping coffee from a paper cup he was gripping with both hands.

Brett told White of Patty's involvement with the Rangers.

"I see," he said after Brett had run it all down.

"I hope you do, Sid. She's not a part of what we're fighting here. In fact, if Patty hadn't stuck her neck out, you'd be directing traffic at the bottom of the ocean right now."

"So what's the plan? You're obviously in charge."

"There is only one way this thing is going to stop. Bandini and Williams must be taken out. I've got a scam going that I hope will bring them both together. If it doesn't then I'll have to think of something else. But we're running out of time. Your life and Jerry's aren't worth a nickel until the Rangers are stopped. There's no doubt that Bandini and Williams pull all the strings. With them gone, the rest of the gang would be like puppets with their strings cut."

"It's an admirable plan, Brett. But let's be honest. You're not the only guy who's thought of taking those guys out. There's been some pretty talented muscle try to pull that off and they've all got one thing in common now: they're dead. They don't take a shit without bodyguards guarding every entrance and exit. Killing Williams's little brother was one thing; he was small time, all mouth. But Poppa and Angie, hell, I just don't know, Brett. You saved my life and I'm thinkin' maybe I could save yours by talkin' you out of committing suicide."

"Thanks Sid, but my mind's made up. I don't have time to explain why I've got to do this, but in a way, I was born to do this. It's all I live for. And if I die trying to undo an injustice or prevent the murder of innocent people, there could be no finer death for me. In fact, for me to turn away from such a situation would be the most humiliating kind of death. No Sid, don't worry. Just try to help if you can, and leave the rest to me. Really. It's all right."

"That's the damnedest bit of philosophy I ever heard, but then you're the damnedest guy I ever met, so maybe it fits."

Just then there were two knocks at the door.

Brett went to the door and said, "Who's there?"

"It's me, Patty."

Brett opened the door and Patty rushed inside.

"Sid," she said moving to his side. "Thank God, you're all right."

"I guess I have you to thank for that. At least partly."

Patty looked up at Brett, wondering how much he had told White about her involvement with Bandini.

"It's okay, Patty," Brett said soothingly.

"But we're not out of the woods yet. Can you stay here with Sid?"

"Sure."

"Good. Then I'll go back to my place, change and try to set the right wheels in motion. But this will be our headquarters. I'll get word back here regularly."

"Why can't Sid go back with you?" said Patty.

"Unfortunately, that's rather obvious," said White. "I'm bought and paid for. As long as the Rangers wield the power, I can't show my face on the street."

Patty looked at Brett and the expression on his face verified what White had said.

"What are the chances you were followed here?" said Brett to Patty.

"It's late enough so there's not much traffic on the street and I was watching. The cab picked me up in front of the building and dropped me at a coffee shop a couple blocks away from here. I know the place; I stop by there sometimes anyhow. Then I went out the back door and walked down a few dark alleys."

"Pretty risky," said White.

"I'm a tough chick," she said and smiled.

"You're smart, too," said Brett and went to the window and looked out into the parking lot. "I'll take the car. You won't be needing it for a while. I'll park it back in your space at the building. Okay, I'd better get going," he said and went to the door.

Patty got up from the bed and went to Brett's side. White excused himself, got up, went into the bathroom and shut the door.

"Yes?" Brett said warmly to the woman standing against his body looking up into his eyes.

"Be careful, honey."

"I will," he said.

"I mean it. You're the hero of this picture. I don't know what Sid and I would do now without you. And I . . . well, I'm a sucker for heroes."

"I've always had a warm place in my bed for beautiful women, too."

Patty smiled.

"Take care of Sid," he said and left.

Patty bolted and chained the door behind him.

Chapter 21

The alarm awakened Brett at nine a.m. He put on his robe and made some fresh coffee. About nine-thirty he called Owen Lang, his banker in San Francisco, and told him that he would need one hundred thousand dollars in cash by noon.

About an hour later Lang called back and told Brett where to pick up the money by one p.m. Brett had been given Lang's name by Yamaguchi. Lang asked no questions. And that was one reason Owen Lang got Brett Wallace's business. He knew there would be unusual transactions and that no inquiries were to be made into those transactions.

"Just see Samual Bower at the First California Bank on Melrose at one this afternoon."

"Thanks Owen. Oh, by the way, have you spoken to Rhea yet?"

"Yes. You know Brett, there are a lot of Japanese restaurants in San Francisco."

"There's only one Rhea. You'll be one of our first customers, Owen. We can discuss my business acumen then. If you see her. . ." Brett didn't know exactly what to say. "Tell her—tell her I said hello."

"Sure. See you soon?"

"Very soon. Maybe we can have lunch next week. We'll talk then. Good-bye, Owen. And thanks again," said Brett and hung up.

Brett tried to put all thoughts of Rhea out of his mind. They would not serve him well now. There was business to be done. And, importantly, Brett knew better than to think of attachments, whether they were lovers or possessions, when he was entering the ring of fire, as Yamaguchi had called it. Such thoughts would cause him to hold back, to care more about the past or the future and distract his total focus from the present. In the ring of fire there was no margin for error. A mistake meant death.

"Hello," a voice said into the phone.

"Angie?" said Brett.

"Brett, good morning," said Angelo Bandini groggily. "Little early, eh?"

"It's a little after ten."

"So, you left early last night. You didn't even stay for the entertainment."

"Entertainment?"

"Oh, nothing special. Just a couple girls I know, they do this act."

Brett said nothing. He portrayed a businesslike manner to the Italian.

"So, I didn't get hold of Mr. Williams last night, but I think I can track him down this afternoon. We can probably meet tomorrow or the next day."

"You and I can meet this afternoon. I'll show you what I said I would. Then we'll meet with Poppa tonight," said Brett firmly.

"Hey, I don't . . ."

"Look, Bandini. I'm a businessman, not a detective agency. You find your partner. I'll keep my end of the bargain this afternoon. Then we deal. Not wait. Otherwise I take my business elsewhere. I'm not a hard-ass, Angie, I just don't like getting jacked around. Either you want to deal or you don't."

"Okay, okay," said Bandini smoothing Brett's feathers. "So you're going to bring the, uh . . . proof with you to lunch?"

"I'm not going to bring it in stuffed in my pockets, Angie, but you'll see it this afternoon. *Before* we meet with Poppa. Where shall I meet you?"

"The Brown Derby on Vine at one."

"One-thirty would be better for me," said Brett.

"One-thirty, paisano. Ciao."

Brett showered, dressed and went downstairs to his car and drove to a phone booth.

"Mr. Summers, please. Room four," Brett said.

"Thank you," said a woman's voice. "I'll put you through."

"Hello?" said another woman's voice tentatively.

"Patty, it's Brett."

"Oh Brett, it's good to hear your voice," she said excitedly.

"Everything all right?"

"Fine. Sid's almost back to normal. I got a deck of cards from the woman at the desk. Said I was your wife," said Patty laughing as she said it.

"I just wanted to see if you were doing okay. Chances are, since no one's bothered you up to now, you're in the clear. But don't do anything foolish. Just sit tight, okay?"

"You're calling the shots, honey."

"Okay, I'll call you later. And take good care of Sid."

Brett hung up and breathed a sigh of relief.

Brett asked the maitre d' at the entrance to the Brown Derby for Mr. Bandini. The man came alive with a smile.

"Mr. Alexander?"

"Yes."

"Follow me, please. Mr. Bandini is expecting you."

The man, dressed in a tux, led Brett to a corner booth where Angelo Bandini sat, sipping on something clear in a short glass.

Bandini smiled widely, "Brett, Brett, good to see you. Sit down, sit down."

Brett sat down, setting a briefcase down next to him, ordered a Perrier, and settled across from the Italian.

"Have you contacted Poppa?" asked Brett as soon as the waiter had taken his order.

"Right to the point, eh? I like that."

Brett said nothing, just stared straight ahead.

"Yes. As a matter of fact I did. And I've got good news." Bandini waited for Brett to play the fool and ask what that news was, but after waiting a few seconds realized such a reply would not come. "Yes, well, I discussed our conversation last night with Mr. Williams. I told him that your main consideration was to see that your money would be in safe, hands—that our organization was not losing control over its territory. Mr. Williams appreciates your concerns, as I do also. So, as an act of faith, we have something very special planned to put your mind at ease tonight. Of course, *after* I see that you are sincere," said Bandini with meaning.

"All right. Let's end the suspense," said Brett and slid the briefcase across the table to Bandini. The Italian clicked the two latches and opened the case under the table on his booth seat. He snapped the case shut and slid it back over to Brett.

"I see that you are a man of your word," said Bandini taking a sip of his drink.

"So, this special treat?"

"Ah yes. Well Mr. Williams said that we could *speak* to you of assurances all night long. But he and I are men of action. And, as they say, a picture is worth a thousand words. So, rather than *tell* you how safe your investment will be, Mr. Williams and I thought we'd *show* you."

"And how might you do that?"

"If you've been keeping up with our exploits in the paper as you say you have, then I'm sure you know who Jeff Archer is."

"The guy whose grandmother was set on fire."

"That's right. Jeff made a futile attempt at revenge against Poppa's younger brother, Terrence, and Terrence had the kid arrested."

"That's old news."

"Terrence was killed a couple days ago and the cops haven't been able to scare up the killer. But we know who it was."

Brett didn't let his eyes betray the tension that had just electrocuted his nervous system. "Oh?"

"Jeff Archer."

"But he was in the hospital under guard at the time of the killing."

"Or so they say. Look, the cops are willing to look the other way about certain things. Archer was freed on his own recognizance the next morning anyhow. We have it on good authority from our people downtown that Archer wasn't in the hospital under police guard the night of the killing. And the modus operandi fits him like a glove. Terrence was hit by somebody who knew how to make the most of a little force.

"Archer was a karate man who already risked his life to kill Terrence. Why not again? And we don't have word from the street that anyone who knew how to use *that* kind of muscle was after Terrence. Put that together with our info regarding Archer maybe not being under guard, and you have a pretty convincing case."

Brett was silent for a moment. He tried to assimilate what he was being told. If Bandini didn't know Brett had killed Terrence Williams, and Brett was almost positive of that, then this really was a show for him. The information Bandini had from downtown obviously wasn't that reliable, but Bandini knew that Brett had no way to verify the facts one way or the other. It was a display of power. The most obvious breach of absolute Ranger power had come with Terrence's death. And this display was meant to seal that breach in a meaningful way. Brett could not argue against the plan, because he had asked for a show of force. And he couldn't very well tell them why he knew they had the wrong man.

"When is this all supposed to take place?"

"Tonight. We'll meet tonight at my place for dinner, just the three of us, and then we'll pay a visit to Jeff Archer."

"What do you have in mind for him?"

"I'll let it be a surprise, but I'll give you a hint—I hope Jeffrey likes the water," said Bandini laughing out loud.

Brett left the Brown Derby about 3 p.m. and drove back to his apartment, carefully watching to see if he was being tailed. He had developed an ability during his Ninja training to sense when he was being followed, even without actually seeing the person following him. He was certain he wasn't being followed now.

Brett had about four hours before his meeting with Bandini and Williams and there wasn't much he could do except wait and meditate.

He thought about trying to track down Archer and warn him, but by the time he did that, it would be too late. And he certainly couldn't risk going to see Archer in person because obviously Archer's residence was under surveillance by Ranger men.

Brett lay down on the couch and relaxed each part of his body slowly and fell into a deep sleep from which he had told himself to awaken at five-thirty p.m.

At precisely five-thirty Brett awoke, put on some music and fixed himself some tea. He showered for the second time that day and dressed well—but casually—in loose fitting clothes that would allow him freedom of movement.

Brett arrived about three minutes before his seven o'clock dinner appointment at Bandini's hillside home, rang the bell, and was shown into the dining room.

There at one end of the table was one of the biggest men Brett had ever seen in his life. Poppa Williams stretched a wide grin across his face and stood up to meet Brett. Williams stood about six-feet-eight—and must have weighed about two hundred and fifty pounds. He was built solidly, like a football player. Bandini, who was seated at Williams's left got up smiling also.

"Mr. Alexander," said the big black man gripping Brett's hand in his own.

"Mr. Williams," said Brett cordially.

"Call me Poppa."

"Brett."

"So Brett, you've made quite an impression on my business partner here. A lot of people don't. Angie says you're a no-nonsense kind of guy. I like that."

"Then we'll get along," said Brett sitting down at the table. The other two did the same.

From where Brett sat he could see two bodyguards almost as big as Williams himself standing on the patio and another bodyguard standing just outside the dining room. And that didn't include the man who answered the door. Brett had had thoughts about taking Bandini and Williams before they all went to see Jeff Archer, but, given the existing odds, decided to wait for a better moment.

"Angie told me you two had a nice lunch," said Williams smiling as though they all knew an inside joke.

"I imagine you're referring to what was inside my briefcase," said Brett.

"That's right," said Williams. Then the smile dropped off

his face and his cold eyes focused hard on Brett. "Now, let's talk."

"Fine. But I've already told Angie what I have in mind."

"That's good. For Angie. Now let's you and me talk, okay," said Williams softly, not taking his eyes off Brett. Brett knew he was being sized up. Williams used his instincts like some people used computers. For Williams they were just as precise.

"First," said Bandini trying to break the icy chill that had frosted the room, "let's have a drink."

The Italian snapped his fingers and the man who had ushered Brett into the dining room appeared. "A martini for myself, a scotch on the rocks for Mr. Williams and . . ." Bandini looked at Brett.

"Vodka. Absolut," said Brett.

The man bowed slightly and left. Bandini made some light small talk while the man was gone. The man returned, served the drinks and left.

"Brett," said Bandini soothingly, "what I think Poppa means is just to run things down for him, you know."

"Yes. I know," said Brett turning his attention toward Williams. "What I'm interested in is making an investment. I've got a great deal of money, cash—it isn't necessary how I came by that money; it's not marked, nor counterfeit. I like money. Lots of it. I'm attracted to the drug business because of its quick and lucrative returns. If one is willing to take the risk. And, like any responsible person, I have done my checking to see which . . . firm, or organization, would be the best one for me to put my money into. Naturally, one cannot go to the SEC or Merrill Lynch to find out that kind of information.

"Until recently, all my research had pointed to the Rangers as the new up and coming organization to back. But, and I told Angie this straight away, recent developments have clouded the issue a little. I'm referring specifically to what's been happening in the Wilshire district."

Williams said flatly, "It's worked to our advantage."

"I would have agreed with you a few weeks ago, before this thing with that old lady. Jesus, setting an old woman on fire. That's a bit much."

A nerve was touched in Williams. Brett knew where the pain was coming from, but pushed the button anyhow.

"That was just plain stupid."

"Look," said Williams, "that incident involved my brother, and now he's dead. So let's not get too excited, okay bro?"

Brett felt the presence of the man just outside the dining room. Obviously he recognized Williams's tone and was ready for action.

"Hey, let's not let this thing get personal. This is business. Come on," said Bandini to the two who sat staring each other down.

"Nothing personal," said Brett breaking the staring match, but not the tension. "I've got something that could be helpful to you, and you've got something that could be useful to me. I'm ready to deal. As soon as I get my assurances about your ability to protect my investment."

Bandini looked across the table at Williams, trying to sense his mood and next move.

Williams looked coldly at Brett. The big man knew he was up against a man who wouldn't back down. Williams was enough of a businessman to realize it wasn't necessary to fall in love with a partner, just so there was mutual benefit. He sensed in Brett an equal. He didn't like him, but he decided he could do business with him.

"Angie told you what I had in mind for tonight?"

"Yes."

"This Archer kid killed my brother. He's still alive. And that's bad for business. Agreed?"

Brett nodded his head.

"So tonight we're going to take out a little ad in the street news. Archer's a dead man. The word will be on the street later tonight. You and Angie and me, we're gonna be there to see Archer go down for the count. Not only will it instruct you as to the ability of our organization to 'protect' its own, it kinda gives us an unsigned pact. You dig?"

Brett understood. Williams was willing to satisfy Brett's demand for a show of strength, but with Brett there as a party to the killing, they were joined together in a binding pact that tied them all to a murder. Brett could not tell the police about the killing without incriminating himself.

"I understand," said Brett.

"Good," said the big man.

"Hungry?" said Bandini to Brett.

"Sure."

Bandini snapped his fingers and the man appeared again. "We'll eat now," Bandini told him.

The man disappeared and within five minutes came back in rolling in a cart and served each man a gourmet dinner consisting of Beef Wellington, an exquisite salad, peas, and an excellent red wine.

"You ever see a man killed before?" Williams asked Brett.

"Once in a fight in a bar," Brett ad-libbed. He certainly couldn't tell him that he had just killed two of their top men the night before.

"How did it make you feel?" asked Williams scooping up a spoonful of peas.

"Didn't make me feel one way or the other. It wasn't me, right?"

Bandini laughed. "You're a hard-ass, Brett. One hard-ass. Don't you think so, Poppa?"

"A regular James Cagney. But a lot of people talk tough. When bullets start flying, then you know."

"I didn't come here to be analyzed or told whether or not I look like John Wayne to you. I came here to do business. That's all. Frankly I don't give a damn what you think about me personally."

Bandini looked at Williams, hoping the black man would keep his cool. He wasn't used to being talked to like that. By the same token not many people offered to put three million dollars into their till. Bandini tried to keep the lid on.

"How long after you see tonight's . . . display do you think it'll be until you turn over the money?" said the Italian.

"If I like what I see tonight, it's ready to be used as needed."

Bandini smiled and sipped his wine.

The three continued to eat in silence for several minutes. Finally Bandini smiled and cleared his throat.

"To success," said Bandini raising his glass.

Brett and Williams raised their glasses and Williams said, "And to honesty among thieves." He looked coolly at Brett and drank half his short glass of Scotch.

The three finished their drinks and made small talk, for which Bandini was thankful. Finally, Williams said, "It's time to go."

Williams and Bandini stood up. As they did the two bodyguards from the patio came inside and walked toward the door. In all, four bodyguards lined up at the door as Bandini, Williams, and Brett prepared to leave. One man opened the door and their two bosses and Brett passed through. Williams went to a late model Cadillac parked in front of the house and got in the back seat. Two of the bodyguards got in the front.

"Brett, you sit back here with me. Angie'll take a second car and follow us."

Angie went to a second Cadillac with the other two bodyguards.

The two cars pulled away and descended down the hill and into the city.

Williams and Brett were silent as they sat in the back seat watching the city roll by outside the window. The two men in the front seat looked straight ahead and didn't talk either.

Finally, Williams reached forward and pulled a clear plastic window closed so that he could talk to Brett in private.

"Angie's really sold on you, Alexander."

"I know."

"I'm not. We might do business because, as you say, we have something the other one wants, but I'm used to a lot more respect than you give me. I've killed people who just *thought* to do what you did tonight."

"Is this supposed to scare me?" said Brett calmly.

"You don't scare. I'm a good judge of character and you're not bluffing. You're genuinely not afraid of me. And, I'll tell you the truth, you're pretty much alone in that category. I don't know why you're not, but that isn't important to me. I respect a man who isn't afraid of me. I don't respect a lotta people. But, like I said, I still don't *like* you. The reason I'm telling you this is because, respect or not, money or not, you play with me the way you did tonight in front of my people and I'll just have them kill you where you stand. It's out of respect I tell you this. You can shine it on, or you can take it as a friendly warning. If we're going to be in business together we don't have to sleep together, but it helps to treat each other right.

"The first part of my life, people didn't treat me like anything but a piece of shit. Then I became a bastard and all of a sudden everybody was smilin' at me and givin' me respect. And I don't get treated like nothin' by no man," said Williams pausing and looking Brett in the eye. "No matter *what*."

The two cars drove west down Sunset through Beverly Hills, Westwood, to the ocean, turned south, and followed the coast highway down into Santa Monica. The moon was full and the moonlight danced like bullets skimming across the waves from the stars all the way to the beach, which was sliding past the car a few feet off the highway.

Poppa Williams said nothing more to Brett during the entire trip and Brett just sat centering himself, getting ready for the challenge. All his training over the last nine years, all the decisions he had made, the skills he had developed, were now going to be tested.

There was only one thing Brett was certain of, and that was that people were going to die in a few moments.

Chapter 22

The Cadillacs pulled up in front of the Sea Gull Motel. It was a one-story structure and housed what looked to be about twelve cottage-type units. A sign blinked off and on and said: "No Vacancy."

That might change quickly, thought Brett.

Angelo Bandini got out of the second car, walked up to the first car and got in the back seat with Williams and Brett.

"Tony and Paulie went to check with Vince. Vince had his eye on Archer all day. It'll just be a few minutes."

"So what do you want me to do?" said Brett addressing Williams.

"Just be there."

Brett didn't say anything.

Just then a man came up to the side of the car. Williams pressed a button and the window slid down.

"I just talked with Vince. Good news," he said.

"This isn't twenty questions, Tony," said Bandini. "What's the story?"

"First, the kid's still in room five. He's by himself. It's almost too easy. Second, we found White."

Brett's heart skipped a beat. Williams's expression flashed real interest.

"Where?"

"In a little dive on Sunset."

"How?"

"We got the boys out in heavy numbers like you ordered and we got lucky. The desk clerk recognized him from his picture in the paper. Guess he was getting a Coke or somethin'. Anyhow when he was at the machine she recognized him."

"How did our man handle it?"

"Just like you ordered, Poppa. He said he was a cop and to keep quiet about the whole thing."

Williams broke out in a coast-to-coast smile. "Now that's the best news I've had in a long time. Tony, take Vince and Paulie with you and finish the business Al and Eddy fucked up last night. And take Vince's car."

"When?"

"Right now. Get going."

Brett swallowed hard. He couldn't let Sid and Patty die, but then he couldn't abandon Jeff Archer either. He had only one choice and that was to speed things up here and race to Hollywood where Patty and Sid sat unaware that killers were coming for them.

"Hey, it's cold. Let's get this thing over with," Brett said to Williams. "What's the hold up?"

"In a hurry? Got a hot date or somethin'?"

"Or somethin'," said Brett flatly.

"No reason to wait," said Williams getting out of the car. Bandini, Brett and the two guys in the front seat did the same.

"We'll all go in together. After Bobby and Teddy," Williams said snapping his fingers and pointing at the two men to lead the way. Then Williams stopped and looked at a Tommy's Hamburger stand twenty yards away from where they stood. "Wait," he commanded his men. "I hate to do something like this on an empty stomach." Williams started to walk toward the stand and Brett's heart sank.

"What . . ." Brett began.

"I'm leading this army and I'm hungry. We march when I say march and we eat when I say eat. That punk ain't goin' nowhere," Williams said finally and the rest followed him to the hamburger stand.

Williams ordered a burger as did his two men. Brett and Bandini just walked around anxiously.

The minutes seemed like hours as the big man downed his burger. All Brett could think about were Williams's men getting closer and closer to the Hollywood motel and walking in on Sid and Patty.

Finally Williams finished and nodded to his men who once again began to lead the way to cottage number five.

The night was cold, with a breeze blowing off the ocean that was only about a hundred yards away. Traffic was light and the only real sound Brett heard was the sound of leather on cement as the five men walked down the sidewalk leading to Archer's cottage.

Bobby and Teddy stopped on either side of door number five and waited for Williams's instructions. Williams nodded to Teddy who then knocked on the door.

A voice answered, "Who's there?"

"The manager," said Teddy.

"What's the matter?" said Archer warily.

"Nothing's the matter, sir. We're just checking the plumbing in your room. The cottage next to yours is having problems and we're trying to find out where the trouble's coming from. Won't be a minute."

There was silence for a moment, then Brett heard a chain fall and a bolt turn. The door opened and Jeff Archer stood framed in the doorway.

Williams stepped forward. "You Jeff Archer?"

"Hey, what is this?" The young man started to close the door, but one of Williams's bodyguards already had his foot in the way.

"My name's Williams. Some people call me Poppa. My brother, for instance, used to call me Poppa. His name was Terrence Williams. Ring a bell, sucker?" said the big man moving closer to Archer.

"Look, I had a run-in with your brother, which I got the worst of. But that's all. I never saw him again."

"That's not what I hear. I hear you killed him. Cornered him in the john at the Cheshire Cat."

"I was in the hospital when he got killed. You've got the wrong man."

"You'll do. If I'm wrong, I'll apologize. But then, it won't do *you* no good, punk," said Williams shoving Archer back into his cottage.

The entire entourage followed, including Brett and Bandini. One of the bodyguards stood by the door. The other closed a window, drew the curtains and turned up the television to try and drown out whatever screams might follow.

"I'm going to kill you myself," said Williams. "But first, son, you be some kinda man, now. You tell Poppa the truth. Tell me you killed Terry. Own up, boy. You're gonna meet your maker. Don't go with a lie on your lips."

Archer looked scared, but didn't cower as Brett thought he might. "You can kill me if you want. But you're wrong about me killing your brother. Not that I didn't want to," he said bravely looking Williams in the eye.

"And I was going to kill you quick," said Williams. "Now it's gonna be inch by inch."

The big man moved forward and punched Archer in the face. But Archer dodged so that most of the blow just glanced off the side of his head. He struck the big man with a punch to the solar plexus and Williams doubled over.

Brett grabbed a pencil from a desk nearby, placed the flat eraser end flush against the palm of his right hand, slid the body of the pencil through the gap between his third and fourth middle knuckles, and closed his fist around it. Teddy and Bobby moved quickly from their positions at the door and window and rushed to their boss's aid. Brett stepped in front of them and, screaming as he did so, punched the pencil once through Teddy's heart and, pulling the bloody instrument quickly out of one wound plunged it into Bobby's heart. Both men fell in their tracks and blood began pumping out of their chests like pulsating geysers.

Bandini's eyes widened and he stood frozen, stunned. No words were necessary. The lines were drawn.

Meanwhile, Jeff Archer was holding his own against Williams, but the big man was starting to get the best of the situation.

Bandini drew a revolver with a silencer on it from his coat pocket and aimed it at Brett. Brett dived behind a chair and dodged the first bullet spat from Bandini's gun. Brett then shoved the chair across the room at Bandini, which made Bandini jump out of the way. Brett anticipated the Italian's movement and tripped him. Bandini went one way, the gun the other.

Bandini sprang at Brett, his hands going for Brett's throat. Brett slapped away Bandini's hands, grabbing him by the back of the head bringing the Italian's head down hard onto his knee. The cracking of bone could be heard across the room and only a single quick groan escaped from Bandini's mouth before his face became a single bloody mass.

Williams looked around and saw the devastation and blood. He grabbed Archer and, using him as a shield, wrapped his forearm around Archer's neck pressing hard against his windpipe causing him to gasp for air.

"Hold it!" yelled Williams, "or I'll snap his neck in two."

Williams stood an entire head taller than Archer, who was just about an even six feet.

"I don't know who the hell you are," said the big man panting, "but you're a dead man now. So is this honky," he said increasing his grasp on Archer.

Brett knew both threats would come true unless he acted immediately. There was only a slight chance, but if he didn't take it, there would be none.

"Okay," said Brett calmly. He slowed the pace, like a magician making the audience look at the other hand. Brett saw Williams relax almost imperceptibly. But Brett saw it and that was enough.

Like a gunfighter with a lightning draw, Brett's hand, in a blur, reached hold of his steel belt buckle, withdrew it and all in a single fluid motion, flipped it at Williams's face. The stainless steel buckle—a five-pointed star the Ninja called a shuriken—passed within inches of Archer's head and found its mark in the middle of the big man's forehead. Williams's eyes bulged, his grip loosened and blood began to trickle down his face. The initial, instantaneous look of surprise was replaced by death's empty stare. By the time Williams hit the ground, he was looking into another world.

"My God!" screamed Archer, not knowing what to think of the man who had just killed four men in his small room. "My God!" he repeated. He was fast approaching a state of shock.

Brett went to the phone beside Archer's bed and dialed the number of the Star Motel.

"Room four. And hurry."

"I'm sorry, sir, but that line is busy."

"This is a matter of great urgency. Please cut in," said Brett frantically.

"I'm sorry, sir, I can't do that," said the woman operator.

"But this is a matter of life and death!"

"I've heard that before. Look, just call back."

One of two things was going on at the motel, Brett deduced. First, the woman was telling the truth and she simply was being arbitrary about not putting the call through. Or secondly, she *knew* what was going on, or about to go on, and was just following orders to not put any calls through.

Brett put the phone down and turned to Jeff Archer. "Listen to me. You're in trouble if you don't. There are four dead men here."

Archer seemed to come around and realize that whoever Brett was, he was a friend.

"What do I do?"

"There's a lot of blood here, but luckily it's all on the floor and the floor is linoleum. I'll bring one of the cars around back and load the bodies inside. Meanwhile, get some towels from the bathroom and start mopping up the blood. Wring the towels out in the bathtub or sink and wash the blood down the drain."

Archer went into the bathroom, came out with two towels and started to work. Brett searched the bodies for keys. He found the set to the car he and Williams came in on Teddy and another set on Bandini.

Brett parked one of the Cadillacs in back of Archer's cottage and loaded two bodies into the trunk and two onto the floor in the back seat. By the time Brett had finished, Archer had cleaned up the floor and was standing at the back door with two bloody towels in his hands watching Brett.

"What about these?"

"Give them to me," said Brett taking the bloody rags. "Here," he said throwing Archer a set of keys. "There's a black Cadillac parked out front. Those are the keys. I'll pull around front and you follow me. And don't touch any part of the car except the door handle and the steering wheel. Got it?"

"Yeah."

"You better. Now let's get going."

Brett drove around to the front and waited for Archer to follow him. They drove down Pico east toward Hollywood.

After about a mile, Brett pulled into a Big Bear Supermarket and drove around back to where several containers were piled high with cardboard boxes, crates, paper, and garbage. He got out of the car, looking around to see if he was being watched, and buried the towels inside some paper, then inside a cardboard box filled with bloody paper used to wrap meats. He got back in the car, pulled onto Pico and continued driving east.

A couple of miles later Brett pulled into a deserted gas station, parked the car in back, and wiped the car of his fingerprints. Then he went to a phone booth near where Jeff was parked waiting for him. He called the Star Motel and got a repeat performance of his earlier conversation.

"Move over," said Brett moving to the steering wheel of the car Jeff was driving. Archer slid over to the passenger side.

"You should be in the clear now, kid," said Brett pulling on to the Santa Monica Freeway.

"You sure?"

"As sure as I can be. Williams's and Bandini's bodies are about as close to their own turf as they are to your place. There's nothing to lead the cops to you."

"But what if they search my room?"

"Why should they? Why would they think you could take on four of the toughest gang fighters in the city at your own place? Maybe you would try to set an ambush, but certainly not at your own motel room. No, they might ask you where you were tonight, but that's about it. It just doesn't make sense to think Williams and Bandini were killed in your motel room. Still, I'd check out of there and go somewhere else pretty soon. Like tomorrow."

"I remember you," said Archer as the two sped along through the night on the freeway. "You were the orderly who asked me where Terrence Williams hung out."

"Good memory."

"So *you're* the one who offed that bastard."

Brett said nothing.

"The man deserved it. I tried to do it myself, but—well, you know the story. You know I've never seen anybody do the kind of things you do. Who the hell are you?"

"There's no time now. I might need your help."

181

"Anything. You name it. What's going on?"

Brett ran down the situation to Archer and finished by saying, "I don't know how many men there will be. I expect a minimum of two and probably no more than four. But that's only a guess. I'll park about a block away and go in from the front. Probably the action will have already moved inside by now. You take the back door and move in slowly, watching and listening to everything."

"This is incredible," was all Jeff Archer could say.

"You're free to walk," said Brett.

"No way."

Brett parked the car on Las Palmas, about a block from the motel, just off Sunset. The two got out and wiped their fingerprints from anything they had touched. Brett pointed to an alley. "That alley runs behind the motel. Count four units from your right; that's the one. Move slowly. Make your senses your antennae. And good luck."

They both smiled at each other and shook hands.

"Thanks," said Archer with meaning.

Brett turned and walked to Sunset, toward the motel.

As Brett approached the motel, he saw the car that Vince, Tony and Paulie had driven away in about a half hour before. He stood still and looked for any guards.

Then he saw a movement. It was the burning ash of a cigarette next to a tree a few feet from the car. A man was standing by the tree having a smoke. As he got closer, Brett recognized the man as Tony, one of Williams's thugs. Silently, Brett approached the lookout. Reaching around from behind, Brett closed off the man's windpipe. Tony tried to spin, but Brett caught him with a chop to the base of the neck and the man collapsed. Brett caught the man before he hit the ground and laid him gently on the grass next to the tree. Brett crushed out the cigarette and scanned the scene again for other guards, until he was convinced there were no others.

Quickly he closed in on unit four. Through a slight opening in the curtains he could see motion and he could hear a sound like whimpering.

Brett wished he could make a more sound judgment, but there was no time left. He had only one high card left to play: surprise.

He went to the front door, stood in front of it for a second, centered himself, breathed deeply, then kicked the door open, diving as he came in.

Three Rangers spun toward him, stunned. Sid White was already bound on the bed. But he was squirming and very much alive. Patty was nude except for her bikini panties. Presumably, the Rangers were getting ready to take a little R and R before doing the dirty work. One man, a black, grabbed Patty, jerked her into the back room and shut the door. The two men left in the room both drew knives. One was a white guy Brett recognized as Paulie, the other a black. And they both came toward him. Brett kicked the knife out of the hand of the black guy and followed the kick through to hit the man squarely on the side of his face, knocking him out cold. Paulie came at Brett in a crouching position, his knife ready to strike out at the right moment. The man lunged. Brett jumped to one side and pushed the man from behind using the man's own momentum. Paulie crashed into the wall head first and collapsed on the floor. Blood began to spread on the floor. In the scuffle the knife had turned and Paulie had run into it when he slammed against the wall.

Now there was silence except for White humming against his gag. Brett moved close to the door of the back room. The element of surprise was gone. Whatever was behind that door was waiting for him. He turned the knob and pushed the door open, not entering, letting the door swing wide.

There, in the middle of the room was the black man standing behind Patty with a knife to her throat.

"I'm walking outta here. Alive. With her," said the man, obviously close to panicking. He held his head beside Patty's and crouched slightly as he spoke.

He moved erratically. Brett wouldn't have a clear shot with the belt buckle.

"Step aside," he said.

Brett did.

The man, still holding the blade to Patty's throat moved past Brett, always facing toward him. He backed out into the living room and toward the open door leading out into the parking lot.

Just as the man and Patty passed through the doorway to the outside, an arm hooked up—and through—the arm wrapped around Patty's neck and sprung the knife hand straight out. Patty dropped to the ground and crawled away. Jeff Archer hooked his arm more securely around the knife arm and used his leverage to whip the man around in a semicircle and finally to his knees. As the man's forehead came down, Archer's knee came up. The forehead and the knee met in a violent collision which left the Ranger out cold.

Brett rushed to Patty, grabbing her dress off the chair as he went.

"Oh Brett," she cried and flung her arms around him.

Archer took the knife from the hand of the man he'd just kayoed and used it to free Sid White from his bonds.

"Jesus! Brett," said White. "I thought I'd bought the farm for sure that time. Who's this?"

Brett looked at Archer and they exchanged looks.

"A friend of mine," said Brett. "Sid get on the horn and call the cops. I'm going to get the hell out of here before anybody sees me. I'd better go out the back."

"Why? Why don't you stay?" said Patty.

"It's a long story. Sid, you tell them you and Jeff handled these guys. Tell them you're both skilled in karate and these guys didn't know what they were in for. If any of these guys come to, which they may not, and say there was another person here, just deny it. It's your word against theirs. Also call Jerry and make sure you get a cop over here who's going to be sympathetic. I'll be at my place. Come by when things get cleared up."

"Me too?" said Jeff Archer.

"You too. Sid and Patty'll show you the way."

Brett turned, went into the back room and disappeared through the back door, down the alley and into the night.

Chapter 23

The next morning Brett had breakfast with Patty, Jeff Archer, and Sid White on his patio. While Brett prepared breakfast inside and Patty and Jeff enjoyed the sunshine outside, Sid White was on the phone getting information from a friend of Jerry Clark's who had a direct line to what was going on downtown.

Brett served omelettes all around, fresh ground coffee, fresh-squeezed orange juice, then sat down and they all waited for White. He came to the table and sat down with a big smile on his face.

"It's happening," said White. "The Rangers are in turmoil. After what happened last night to Bandini and Williams, plus the fact that we successfully freed ourselves from Ranger thugs, all hell is breaking loose. It seems that besides what's been happening in the Wilshire district, there have been a lot of cases pending against the Rangers. But, with the kind of control the Rangers exerted—until last night—naturally nobody wanted to testify. But all that's changing. Cases are being reopened all over the place. And since the leadership of the Rangers is in doubt, no one is issuing any orders. In short, they're through. Word is, even Ranger lieutenants are hitting the road in a hurry before warrants are issued for their arrests.

"To you," said White to Brett.

Jeff, Patty and Sid raised their juice glasses and clicked them against Brett's. Brett nodded, smiled, and they all drank.

"Looks like things are going to be safe around here. I

know I'm going to feel more secure with you around," said Patty.

Brett smiled and said, "I'm leaving today."

"But . . ." she started.

"I've accomplished what I set out to do. I'm done. Besides, the neighborhood believes that it was successfully defended by its *own* people, not some outside superman. That means a lot. This is a turning point. Let it start from here and you all keep that spirit alive after I leave."

The fact that he was leaving answered a lot of other questions Patty would have asked. Still, she was grateful.

After breakfast the gathering broke up. Patty was the first to leave. At the door she put her arms around Brett tightly and looked up into his eyes. "Thanks," she said. "You're the closest thing I've ever known to a hero, Brett Alexander, or whatever your name is. I'll never forget you."

"I'll never forget you, either. We'll see each other again some time," he lied. "I'll look you up the next time I'm in town."

Patty said nothing, just kissed him lingeringly on the mouth for the last time and left.

"Nice servin' with you, son," said White gripping Brett's hand firmly as he stood at the door ready to exit. "I wish you could stay. But I won't even ask. You know my door is always open. You got yourself a friend if you ever need one. Good luck," said White and left.

Brett came back into his living room to find Jeff Archer sitting on the couch.

"So what are your plans?" said Brett sitting down in a chair opposite his guest.

"I haven't any," he said looking Brett in the eye.

"Oh," said Brett casually.

"What the hell do you do anyway?"

"Whatever I want," said Brett smiling.

Archer broke out in a smile. "I'd like to go with you."

"That's impossible. But then, you already know that," said Brett dismissing the notion.

"But I don't have any family left. My grandmother was it. She raised me and sent me through school. I finished college last year and haven't been doing much for the past few months. I was looking for a job, but I couldn't find one. I graduated in business at Santa Barbara University. And I'm good at it. I could run a business. I worked for a friend's father the last four summers and by last summer I was pretty much running his organization. And just before I came here I was working part-time teaching kung fu at a dojo up in Santa Barbara. I'm not bad at that either."

"So I noticed."

"Nothing like you, but then I've never seen—hell I've never even *heard* of—anyone as good as you. Any comparison to you isn't really fair.

"Look, I've got no ties. I'm eager to work and I'll bet you could use somebody like me. And I proved myself to you, didn't I?"

"You're a little too cocky for me," said Brett grinning a little.

"But I can learn. From the *best*. And man, you *are* the best and we both know it. It'd be as exciting as hell."

"I *could* use somebody to monitor my business affairs on a daily basis, but no, no, it's out of the question."

"When do I start? You're leaving today you said. I'll just pick up a few things and I'll be ready," said Archer.

"Look, Jeff, I like you and I wish you all the best, but your coming with me is simply out of the question. Impossible. And I don't want to talk about it any more. And that's final."

Chapter 24

"This is some view," said Jeff Archer sitting down at the table on Brett's deck overlooking the bay and San Francisco.

"Speaking of beautiful views, this is Rhea," said Brett indicating the beautiful Oriental woman to his left. She nodded.

"And this is Jeff Archer," said Brett to Rhea. "Jeff's going to be handling my business affairs and running a dojo I plan to open in Sausalito."

"Pleased to meet you, Rhea. Brett told me how beautiful you were."

"You did?" she said to Brett.

He just smiled.

"But," Jeff continued, "I wasn't prepared for anyone as beautiful as you actually are."

Rhea smiled and said, "Brett, I get a very good feeling from this young man."

"I'll drink to that," said Brett lifting his glass, through which he could see the city glistening.

The three raised their glasses and touched them together softly. Brett said, "To a long and fruitful partnership; and may we always be the best of friends."

Glasses clinked. Knowing looks were exchanged. The team was formed.

MEN OF ACTION BOOKS
NINJA MASTER
By Wade Barker

The Ninja Master is Brett Wallace, San Francisco partner in the hottest Japanese restaurant in town and a martial-arts studio. He marries a beautiful Japanese woman and begins to take over his father's real-estate business—when tragedy strikes. His pregnant wife and parents are savagely murdered by a hopped-up motorcycle gang—and the killers escape justice when their case is thrown out of court on a technicality.

Revenge becomes Wallace's career. He brings his own form of justice to the killers and then escapes to a secret Ninja camp in Japan to become a master in the deadly craft. Armed with a new identity, he roves the world bringing justice to people who have been wrongfully harmed and whom the legal system has failed. From slavers in South Africa to bizarre religious cults to the Chinese Mafia, the Ninja Master is feared and revered as he combines a talent for modern justice with an ancient art of killing.

NINJA MASTER #1: VENGEANCE IS HIS
(C30-032, $1.95)
NINJA MASTER #2: MOUNTAIN OF FEAR
(C30-064, $1.95)
NINJA MASTER #3: BORDERLAND OF HELL
(Coming in February) *(C30-127, $1.95)*